Locked Up

Locked Up

Cristy Watson

James Lorimer & Company Ltd., Publishers
Toronto

Any errors or misrepresentations are wholly the responsibility of the author.

James Lorimer & Company Ltd., Publishers acknowledges funding support from the Ontario Arts Council (OAC), an agency of the Government of Ontario. We acknowledge the support of the Canada Council for the Arts, which last year invested $153 million to bring the arts to Canadians throughout the country. This project has been made possible in part by the Government of Canada and with the support of Ontario Creates.

Cover design: Tyler Cleroux
Cover image: Shutterstock

Library and Archives Canada Cataloguing in Publication

Watson, Cristy, 1964-, author
    Locked up / Cristy Watson.

(SideStreets)
Issued in print and electronic formats.
ISBN 978-1-4594-1403-7 (softcover).--ISBN 978-1-4594-1404-4 (EPUB)
    I. Title. II. Series: SideStreets

PS8645.A8625L63 2019   jC813'.6   C2018-905311-9
                                                   C2018-905312-7

Published by:
James Lorimer &
Company Ltd., Publishers
117 Peter Street, Suite 304
Toronto, ON, Canada
M5V 0M3
www.lorimer.ca

Distributed in Canada by:
Formac Lorimer Books
5502 Atlantic Street
Halifax, NS, Canada
B3H 1G4

Distributed in the US by:
Lerner Publisher Services
1251 Washington Ave. N.
Minneapolis, MN, USA
55401
www.lernerbooks.com

Printed and bound in Canada.
Manufactured by Friesens Corporation in Altona, Manitoba, Canada in December2018.
Job # 250170

This book is dedicated to one family whose courage and humility know no bounds. From tragedy they created new, strong bonds and continue to this day to inspire and support others. And one family member, in wanting to give back to the community, is forging a new path. This is not their story; however, I wrote this novel to celebrate what they taught me about the incredible gifts of forgiveness and understanding. Thank you to this amazing family for sharing your journey and your light!

Chapter 1

Nightmare

My life is stuck on repeat of one day. The one day I can't take back. The one day I can't change.

And the memory is with me all the time.

It was the middle of December and the temperature had dropped. We'd just had a huge dump of snow. The kind of snow cities like Edmonton, Toronto, and New York get. The kind of snow that cripples a city. In Vancouver it was even worse because we weren't used to snow.

That morning, I woke up to notifications blowing up my phone. Dad was in the car, texting me that he was driving his latest girlfriend to work. That meant I had to get to school on my own. His next texts said I needed to walk my dog, Gemini, do the dishes, and shovel the sidewalk, all before leaving the house. Like that was going to happen! Instead, I hit the snooze button and curled up under the covers to get warm.

Then I ended up being so late I didn't have time to walk Gemini. I didn't have time to do any of the things Dad had asked me to do. Instead, I showered, wolfed down my breakfast, and ran out the door. Halfway down the block I was sorry I hadn't grabbed my scarf. Tiny shards of ice pricked my skin.

I remember glancing at my phone and seeing that the first bell was going to ring in ten minutes. If I got another late slip, they'd call home. Last thing I needed was more attitude from my dad, even if it was his fault. I passed this old car that was idling to warm up the engine, and got a great idea. I'd get to school faster if I took it. Who cares that I wasn't legally allowed to drive at fifteen?

The car door was unlocked. My dad had ditched me, and this seemed like fate. So I jumped in. My heart was pounding, like Bachi sticks banging against my Taiko drum. Adrenaline seemed to funnel right down to my foot. Before I knew what was happening, I had pressed the gas pedal to the floor, turned the steering wheel hard, and pulled out into the street. Normally the tires would have screeched, but the bank of snow made it hard to peel out. So the only sound in the deep silence of Vancouver was the running engine and the crunch of tires on snow.

And my racing heartbeat.

The car tires slid into the ruts in the snow formed by vehicles that had left earlier in the morning. I didn't push the car too hard because I didn't want to spin out. I had loads of time to change my mind. I could get out of the car and leave it at the nearest curb.

But I didn't.

Instead I drove toward my high school, wishing I had my own wheels. If I did, I could surprise this girl I liked. With my own car, maybe I'd be cool enough that Tanika would go out with me. With my own car, maybe I'd be brave enough to ask her out. I'd pick her up and she'd settle in close. Then we'd ditch school for the day and hang out.

But I was pulled from my daydream as the car slipped in the snow. And my heart stopped when I scanned the mirrors and spotted the cop car behind me.

I don't know why, but I was sure he knew I had taken the car for a joy ride. Panic pressed my foot onto the gas pedal. Ahead was a street that led away from the main road. I thought I could lose the police car. But as I turned the steering wheel and revved the gas, I hit a sheet of black ice. The car slid sideways.

I wrenched the steering wheel and pounded the brakes. The old car didn't have anti-lock brakes. I felt a burn through my arms. Nothing I did worked to control the vehicle. I was sliding straight toward a telephone pole.

And between me and the pole was a guy in a green jacket.

I closed my eyes. There was a popping crunch as the car hit the pole.

Someone screamed.

A buzz rang through my ears. I sat stunned like a bird that's flown into a window. Every part of me was vibrating. It took a few moments for me to figure out what had happened. But those moments felt like hours.

I wiped my eyes with the sleeve of my jacket. In front of the headlights was a red scarf on the white snow.

Right.

There had been a man.

My breakfast heaved out onto the car seat. I couldn't find the courage to get out of the car to check on the guy on the sidewalk. His dangling red scarf billowed in the wind.

When I finally opened the door, people had gathered on the street. One person had hurried to the front of the car and bent down between the telephone pole and the car. Others stared at me with accusing glares.

I took a deep breath because I felt like I might pass out. The air chilled right down to my lungs. I inched toward the front of the car but was jostled sideways as someone knocked into me. He yelled for me to call 911. I pulled out my cell phone, but my hands were shaking and the phone dropped into the snow and disappeared. It felt like the temperature had dropped too — like, twenty degrees. I was shaking so hard I had to reach out for the hood of the car to keep my balance.

Sirens wailed. The snow by the front tire was dripping with crimson. I steadied myself as a second wave of nausea hit.

"Get out of the way," hollered another stranger. The ambulance staff knocked into me as they rushed by and I fell into the embankment. As my head lolled to the side, I remember looking directly at the man I had hit.

Then everything went black.

Just the way it does every time I remember that morning.

✻✻✻

I don't dream when I sleep. It's when I open my eyes that the nightmare begins. It's been two and half years since the day I jumped in that car and took off for school. But every day since then has been the same.

I wake up in a pool of sweat. My shirt is plastered to my back. My heart races and my whole body shakes. Everything that happened that day is in front of my eyes. The smashed car, the red scarf blowing in the wind, the eyes staring at me as I lie in the snow.

Chapter 2

Inside

In the morning, it always takes me a while to shake off the images. Today, it's even longer than usual before I can take a deep breath. I look down at my legs and see I have been pounding them with my fists. They are full of red marks. One spot is going to sport a bruise. I'll just keep my sweats on during gym class.

A sigh escapes my throat as I sit up. The bed creaks with the shift in my weight. It's not like I'm heavy like Macaroni, whose room is next to mine. My bed just creaks because it's old and cheap. I don't know Macaroni's real name, but he got his nickname in here because he loves mac and cheese. Unlike Macaroni, I'm average — average height, average weight. Not skinny like Wired, another guy in here. But if I was, I might be able to slide through the slats in my window, right out of this joint.

Before flipping the covers off, I knock on the wall twice. It's my way of saying hi to Macaroni. I'm not sure why I bother. He's the only guy lower in the pecking order than I am.

The floor is cold when my feet land on it. I walk across the room and grab my clothes. Today is green day. I switch my pyjama bottoms for a pair of green sweats. I miss my Def Leppard T-shirt, my Canucks ball cap, and my favourite black jeans. Now I wear the same clothes as everyone else. And the same colours, depending on the day.

I flop back down on my bed and wait.

＊＊＊

There's a spider who sits in the corner of my room, above the desk I use for school work. I spot her sitting in her web. My first week in here, I kept breaking her web. I couldn't stand having her watching me. Judging me. So, every day, I'd knock down her home. And every day, she'd rebuild it. She never gave up.

After a while, I stopped ruining her world and gave her a name. She's inside, like me. The only things growing on the grounds here are weeds. So that's what I called her, Weed.

Sometimes I forget and talk to her out loud. One time it got me patted down by the guard. Without thinking, I said something like, "Weed, you're going to help me get through the day, right?"

Now the spider has become a joke with the other guys.

"Where's the weed?"

"Did you bring weed with you?"

It's a bad joke. But my first week in, it made it easier to get to know the guys.

Weed and I are stuck in this room. And we're both stuck in a day that goes on forever in the exact same way.

I make my bed and then Collins, my correctional officer, comes in to check my room. He gives me the "all clear" for my morning to begin. Now I am allowed to go to the cafeteria. I give Collins a weak smile. It's 7:00 a.m.

As I walk to breakfast, Collins stays by my side like a bodyguard. Only he's not here to protect me. It's the other way around. He's here to be sure I don't do anything wrong. He's really called a peace officer, but we call them COs because that would be their title in regular prison. And while they call this a youth custody centre, it's being locked up all the same.

I scan the cafeteria as soon as I walk in. Macaroni is by himself at the side table. It's like his assigned seat. Wired is sitting at one of the long tables near the back. Like everyone else in here, his nickname fits. He's tapping his foot and drumming his fingers on the table.

As always, the food line is jammed, shoulder to shoulder. Just as I get my plate loaded, a guy knocks my elbow. My tray slips out of my hands. The food slides off and lands in a messy heap on the floor.

"Clean that up!" yells a CO.

The guy who knocked into me is a Diablo, from the gang in here. I grab a grimy cloth, bend down, and clean up the food. Then I go to the back of the line and start all over again.

By the time I get a fresh plate of food, the tables are packed. I shuffle over to where Wired is sitting and park myself across from him. He is shovelling the slop from his plate into his mouth like it's the best stuff on earth. Between mouthfuls he says, "Did you hear that Strummer got caught again? He's off to the big joint. There's no way he's coming back to juvie. Isn't he like, twenty-one?"

"Yup." My throat tightens. "I was a wreck when I first got here. Strummer helped me to chill. Remember how he used to borrow a guitar from the staff and jam? He did a wicked rendition of the riffs for 'Hotel California.'"

"Yeah," says Wired. He sings a few bars. "And just like in the song, we checked out the minute we got here, but none of us can leave."

I nod my head. I was right to worry about how Strummer would make it on the outside. If Strummer can't make it, how the hell am I going to survive when I get out?

"How long was he in here?" Wired runs a piece of toast through the yolk on his plate.

"Six years. He talked about how out there, you have to face all your demons. Everything that put you in here is still out there. Maybe Strummer just couldn't cut it. Freedom. Choices. So much time to fill." I shudder just thinking about it.

"Wasn't he the one who named you Strider, instead of Kevin?"

"Yeah. We're both into *The Lord of the Rings*. Strummer thought the description of Strider fit me. But I'm not anything like Strider. I'm not fierce or loyal, and I'm definitely not good with a sword!"

Wired shakes his head. "Well, Strummer messed up. When I get out, I plan on getting it right. I'm staying out. I hate this place."

I lay into him. "But you did shit that got you in here."

"You mean I got caught doing it."

"What's the difference?"

Wired laughs. It's no use talking to him about this stuff. He works the system. And he makes the system work for him. If he gets out, he'll be sure not to get caught next time.

I push the food around on my plate. Nothing makes it look appealing.

Wired chomps on his last piece of toast. Then he reaches across the table with his plastic fork and starts in on my food. "So I'm still in loads of crap here," he says. "That stunt I pulled last week got me in deep. I lost all my privileges."

"Except for meals. You still have those," I snort. He's just about cleared my plate. I grab the last piece of toast and shove it in my mouth.

"Yeah, but now I have to figure out another way to get the goods inside."

Wired gets smokes and booze for anyone who is willing to pay. Sometimes he gets harder stuff too.

"Screw up and you'll be in secure custody again," I remind him.

"I've got a handle on things. But I need to borrow some cash. Lend me fifty bucks to get through the week."

"What, you think I'm loaded? Your dad gives you extra money for the canteen each month. It's not my fault you screwed up and lost access to it."

"So what are you saving all your money for, anyway?" he snarls.

"None of your business."

"Whatever! Hand over a little now. You'll get more back in the long run."

"Damn it, Wired! What part of NO did you miss?" I slam my tray down.

Wired stands and pushes his tray toward the centre of the table. "Sometimes you can be a real asshole, Strider." He shoves a chair as he leaves the room.

In the year Wired has been in, I have discovered that he doesn't like to hear the word *no*. Out there he was used to getting his way. As I place both our trays on the counter, I feel eyes on me. I turn my head and see that some members of the Diablos just witnessed our interaction. I put my head down and clear out of the cafeteria.

Chapter 3

Visitors' Day

It's Saturday and my dad is coming to visit. When I know Dad's coming it's like I can't breathe. Collins arrives to take me to the visitors' area. It's blue day today, so I'm wearing blue sweats.

I arrive in the visitors' area before my dad. There are six tables with four chairs at each one. The candy and drink machines are against the far wall, opposite the door where they let people into the room.

Collins has to supervise all visits. So he waits off to the side while I grab a Coke from the machine and wait for my dad at an empty table. Dad is late, as usual. Given that we don't get much time as it is, it always pisses me off. After another ten minutes of waiting, a whiff of after-shave lets me know that Dad has arrived.

"Funny how you show up when it's time to *leave*," I say. I turn my chair backwards and lean my arms on the back of it, putting a barrier between me and my dad.

"I don't know why I bother coming," Dad says. "All I get is attitude." He stands, looking lost.

I gesture for him to sit down. He glances around the room, which is busy with other visitors. He grabs a chair and rests his hands on the table. Then the long silence begins. This is how it plays out every time. We sit in silence for most of the visit. My dad keeps his head low and moves his clasped fingers in and out. I stare at his balding head. Other than the hushed voices of the rest of the visitors, the only sound is me slurping my Coke.

This time, Dad surprises me by being the first to break the silence. In my two and half years of being in, he's never done that before.

"So I'm not good at putting my thoughts into words," he says in a quiet voice. "But the other day I was walking Gemini down at Second Beach. You know how he loves to run? Well, he was pulling on his leash and practically yanking my arm out when I realized . . ."

I can picture my dog and all the times I used to run with him. Suddenly I'm pissed at my dad. The words come flying out of my mouth. "What the hell? The one thing I miss most about being in here is my dog. And *that's* what you decide to finally start talking about?"

People at the other tables stop talking and stare in our direction. Collins has crossed his arms over his huge chest. He looks at me and raises an eyebrow.

"How am I supposed to know what topics are off-limits?" says Dad. "How come whenever I come here I feel like *I'm* the one who's on trial?"

"I don't know." My thoughts are all jumbled in my head. I can't figure out what to say. Maybe that's why my dad gets quiet. I only know I feel like it was his fault. He's why I took the car and got into this mess.

Dad looks at the other visitors. He lowers his voice and says, "I don't have to come see you. I don't have to spend time here. I missed going ice fishing with my buddies from work. They went to Sheridan's cabin at the lake. But where did I go today? Oh, to see my son. Who never talks to me, unless it's to give me attitude."

Now my brain is on fire. "So go to the stupid cabin. I'm just some check mark on your to-do list, anyway." I stand and lean over the table, spewing hot words in my dad's direction. "You know I wouldn't have gotten in that car if you had just driven me to school. Instead, you cared more about someone who was only around for a few days. Like always."

"Oh, so this is my fault now? You really think I'm the reason you're stuck in here?"

I sit back down and shake my head. It was his fault that day. And he's the reason Mom left. If he'd only been more interested in my life, maybe things wouldn't have gotten so screwed up. My thoughts must show in my facial expression, because Dad takes one look at me and stands up.

He's skinnier than the last time I saw him. His clothes are rumpled and have stains on them, like he forgot to do laundry. I watch as he stretches one arm into the sleeve of his jacket. Then the other arm. That means we're done for today. That means whatever else I have to say needs to wait until the next time I see him.

Dad walks away and opens the door to leave the visitors' room. I quickly call out, "You were saying something about Gemini. Is he okay?"

Dad's words follow him out the door. "He's fine."

The visit is over. I watch as the door shuts behind him. The door that leads outside. The door that takes him home. Home to my dog.

The walk back to my room is slow. Back there, I am pissed that things went south so fast with my dad. I bang my head against the wall.

Macaroni knocks back.

✳✳✳

It's been three days since the blow-up with my dad. Today I have to see my parole officer at two o'clock. Just like with Collins, it's not his real title. Jackson's real title here is probation officer, or PO, but we refer to our release as parole. Just because we're younger doesn't mean our time here is any different from a prison stint.

Before I meet with Jackson, I have chores to finish. This week I'm stuck cleaning up the gym. It reeks of sweat and dirty socks. And with no open windows, the stale air just gets recycled. As I walk back to the common area, I spot Wired headed straight for me.

"Strider," he says. "Glad we bumped into each other. About that loan . . ."

I don't have time for this. "Look, I'll think about it, okay?"

"Well don't think too hard! A few Diablos aren't happy they're having to wait for their goods. And I have my meeting with Jackson coming up. He's been on my case about school. So you're going to help me study as repayment for holding out!"

Crap. So not only is Wired threatening me with the gang members, but I also forgot we have a Grade Twelve History exam coming up. "Give me a couple of days to get my work done for the other classes. Then I'll help you out."

He agrees to give me *one* day. I sigh in

relief as Wired struts down the hall. I have managed to stall him for now. But it won't last. I feel like if I help him out, I'm partly to blame for whatever happens to people who buy his stuff. Just before I came to juvie, there was a kid here who died of an overdose. The guy was only seventeen. Like me. Strummer told me about him and it freaked me out.

I pass the bulletin board with activities we can sign up for. Tomorrow afternoon there will be a creative writing session. That would keep Wired out of my way for a while. He'd never go for anything extra that feels like school work.

It looks like some writers want to share their talents with us. *Whatever*, I think. I'm not into poetry or reading. But I do like listening to music and playing Taiko drums. If Strummer were here, he'd go for the song writing session. Before I lose my nerve, I add my name to the list.

Then I return to my room while I wait for Jackson.

Chapter 4

Meeting with Jackson

I always end up thinking about the future when I meet with Jackson. It makes sense, because that's what we talk about. That's his job. He has to get to know me to help determine if I am ready for any kind of life beyond here. But he doesn't know my plan. He has no idea that I am scared shitless of a life beyond here.

At 2:00 I head to the visiting area. Jackson is waiting with two Cokes and a bag of barbeque chips for me, and a chocolate bar for himself. He's wearing jeans and a dress jacket. His grey hair just touches the tops of his ears and his grin shows a crooked row of teeth. I'm not full of tension, like I was on my dad's visit. It's easier with Jackson, since he always starts the conversation.

"Hey kid," he says, as I grab a chair. "How's the studying going?"

I shrug.

We have four classes a day so we can finish grade twelve. I'm mostly blowing off the coursework. If I fail, they may keep me in longer. And that suits me just fine.

Jackson's breath smells like onions. "I'm sorry to hear that Strummer re-offended. I know you two got along."

"Yeah, it sucks. If he can't make it out there, how will I cope?" I'll prime Jackson slowly so my plan will make sense to him.

"Most of the young people in here are just like you. They're scared of the future. But they're still doing the work to get out of here and get back into society. Is something holding you back?"

"I don't know. Guys like Wired seem to only care about getting out. They don't think about what it will be like out there. It's easy for guys like him."

"I don't know about that. But we're not here to talk about Wired. We're here to sort out what you need. What's going to help you?"

"Well, I'm going to that writing thing tomorrow."

"Yeah, I saw that you signed up. That's good. I didn't know you were into writing."

I'm not, I think. *But I need to be as far away from Wired as possible.* Out loud I say, "Yeah. Strummer and I knocked out some lyrics for a song he was working on when he was in here. Maybe I can finish his song?"

"This is good, Kevin."

When Jackson says my real name, I shiver. I hardly ever hear it. And when I do, it's mostly from Jackson or my dad. Will I ever get used to hearing it again?

Jackson continues, "How are your studies going? Final exams are coming up. Are you ready?"

"Hey, when I was out, I wasn't into studying. Why should things be different now? I just want to do my time."

"Okay . . . but I think you're pretty bright and it seems like you're not working up to your potential. Find a way to put in an effort over the next few months and pull your grades up. It will be worth it."

I look at Jackson and his smile betrays more of his lunch. "How?"

"It looks like you may be up for early probation!"

"*What?*"

"Yeah. You've kept your head down. You've stayed out of trouble. Heck, you've even managed to keep Wired at bay. That's a feat in itself!"

My voice is loud when I reply. "I . . . never thought with what I did I would ever be granted early parole." The room shrinks and I feel pressure squeeze my head. "You don't really think I will get out early, do you?"

"When you were sentenced they gave you the maximum to make a point. Joyriding gets less than two years, but because there was a person harmed during the crash, they gave you five. You took the anger management course I suggested last fall. And now you've signed up for this writing workshop. I think you're on the right track. Do you need a tutor to help with your studies?"

"Naw . . . I've got this." I stand and push my chair back.

Jackson gets up from his seat and picks up our empty pop cans. "Listen. There's one more thing before you go."

I'm backing up toward the door to make a quick exit. I've heard enough of this crap about early parole. It has me shaking.

"There may be someone new on your list of visitors," says Jackson. "She hasn't been approved yet. But I believe she can help you move forward. Help with your probation. I'll keep you posted."

I turn my back on Jackson as I reach the door. I hear the other door close, meaning he has left the room, and I turn so I can see him. He's looking through the window at me. I don't know why, but for the first time, he reminds me of my dad. I push through my door and past the guard. My feet are half-running along the hallway back to my room. I fly in the door and plop face first onto my bed. The door slams shut behind me. I am locked in once again. Just me and my thoughts.

Only this time, the words EARLY PAROLE are on my tongue. And the taste is bitter.

How could I possibly have earned a chance for early parole?

I know I screwed up. I don't *want* to be

released. Look at how that turned out for
Strummer. I have to figure something out so
I can finish my full time in here. When I was
sentenced, I only got to see the wife of the guy
I hit. I never had to face anyone else. Except
my dad. And that was bad enough.

I remember my dad's rage that day. I
can still see the look on his face. Most young
offenders go home the first night they are
caught. But my dad didn't want me at home.
His words still roll around in my head. He told
the social worker, "Keep him. I don't
want him."

So I was put in a special foster home that
night. The family gave me dinner and a bed.
I ended up staying with them until a bed was
ready here. I had loads of time to think about
what I had done. Too much time.

Now, two and a half years later, I am used
to this joint. There isn't anything out there for
me, anyway. So why bother?

Getting out isn't on my roster.

"Weed, you're used to being in too, aren't you?" I roll over and look at my spider. "Out there you'd have to deal with crappy weather. Rain and wind blowing you around. You'd have animals knocking into your web. Here, it's the same every day, now that I leave you alone." I prop my pillow behind my head and sit up.

"I'm not sure what keeps you going in here, Weed. But it's still got to be easier than living on the outside."

Of course, Weed doesn't answer me. My eyes close.

Then I am back in the car, driving in deep snow.

Chapter 5

Changing The Story

When it is time for that creative writing thing, Collins collects me. We head to the common area.

Macaroni is already there and signals for me to sit with him. I'm usually the only one who ever talks to him. As I flop into the chair beside him, he's smiling like it is Christmas morning. Like he's not stuck in here.

"Well, aren't you excited?" he asks. "I can't wait to check out the slam poetry. I brought along some poems, in case they want to hear them." He pulls out a ratty old book with ripped corners and flips through it. I hope he isn't planning to read one out loud while we are waiting. I scan the room so Macaroni won't think I'm his audience.

The place is more packed than I expected. Four COs are leaning against the wall. In front of us a low table has been set up. Behind it three people sit, shuffling papers and talking with each other in whispers. This is the first time the creative writers have been in here. The slim guy, who looks to be about thirty, stares at us. He's taking us in. He's wondering what crimes we've committed and how safe he is in here.

Lucky that Luke and Dex aren't around. Luke killed a guy and Dex was running guns and breaking in to people's homes. He beat up one guy so badly the dude almost died. You wouldn't expect that from guys who are still years away from their twenties. But it's real. As if the dude at the table can hear my thoughts, his shoulders hunch. He picks up the book in front of him and buries his head in it.

Since the writers are here for everyone, girls are in the room too. Other than for a couple of classes, all of us rarely get to do things together in here. And when we are together in a room, we can't sit beside each other. That must be why there are so many guards here today. They want to make sure we don't get too close. Wired was into a girl here last year and they were caught kissing. That's it. Just lips pressed to lips. But the whole joint was on lockdown for two hours. It sucked! It's times like that when the guards give us attitude and make our lives hell.

I was kind of into one of the girls my first year in. But we could never get together, so I gave up. None of them are like Tanika, anyway. Or what I figure Tanika would be like if I'd had a chance to get to know her better. She's probably getting ready for graduation. I bet she's even more beautiful now. If my life were different, I would definitely be asking her to go with me to the grad dance.

"Let's get started," says a folksy-bluesy voice, bringing me out of my thoughts. "We are thrilled to be here today," says the woman. "We used to visit the local prison and did a lot of work with adult inmates. We hope to get that gig again, but we're lucky to have this opportunity to connect with all of you."

Connect with us? It sounds like we're blocks of Lego. I'm beginning to regret my decision to come here. I'm cursing Wired under my breath.

The woman speaks again. "We're going to introduce you to the writing professionals who are here today. Then we'll talk about writing in general, before moving into smaller groups. As you noticed when you signed up, we'll have fiction, poetry, and song writing. We hope you're as excited as we are."

A few girls nod their heads. Macaroni has a

wide grin on his face. I bet I look totally out of place.

The woman introduces the panel. The guy who is sitting at the end is the songwriter. His name is Sean. He's still studying us but smiles when he is introduced. The poet is named Keto, and he's into slam poetry. The woman's name is Kendra and she writes novels. She pays homage to the founder of the program here in BC, where writers connect with inmates. Even though I came just to get away from Wired, I admit it is cool to have people from the outside caring about us. Sometimes it feels like no one even knows we're here.

Kendra stands and smoothes her skirt. "I've written nine novels. One of them is aimed at people in their twenties. That's pretty close in age to many of you. My character, Elsie, has a tough life. I'm thinking some of you can relate to that?"

Some of us? All of us know tough, being in here.

Kendra begins a slow walk back and forth in front of our rows of seats. "The beauty of being a writer is that *we* create the stories. We make up lives for our characters. We get our characters in trouble and then we give them tools to get out of trouble."

"Are you saying you can *write* us right out of this joint?" one of the girls asks. I hear people snickering.

"Sort of. I can't write you out of here. But YOU can."

More people chuckle. They aren't buying it.

Kendra continues. "As writers, we determine where our characters go and how they get there. You may not be able to leave here for some time. But you can write your journey. Or maybe you write about what life could be like outside of here. Then you find a way to make that happen. It's really that simple. And over the next four sessions, we'll show you how to do it."

It's really that simple.

Nothing in life is simple. That much I figured out on the day I took that car. But it would be nice to believe things could change. That we could have the power to make things change.

When we break into small groups, Macaroni goes with the slam poet. I hang with Sean.

He plays his guitar and sings one of his original songs and then talks about his process. "Sometimes I get the lyrics first," he says. "And sometimes the music comes to me before the words."

One of the girls jumps in, "I have no trouble writing lyrics. But I can't always get the notes down. Do you ever have trouble with that? What do you do when that happens?"

I think about Strummer and his song.

"Yeah," agrees Sean. "Of course it's cool when the two come together. But I have days where I can't knock out the words, no matter how hard I try. Then I decide not to push it. To let it just happen. I have tunes rolling around in my head all the time, but the lyrics take more work for me. That was a good question. Anyone else have questions?"

I hope he doesn't expect all of us to share. I wouldn't know what to say. I don't have a process, since I don't write songs. But Strummer and I jammed and talked about music. I wish he was here right now. He'd be telling us all how he gets his ideas. I wonder if Strummer has access to a guitar in prison. I wonder how he is surviving in there.

Hanging with Sean is making me miss Strummer even more.

But at least I am killing an hour without having to deal with Wired.

Chapter 6

Pressure

I wake up the same way as always. But this time, I notice my legs are already red. It looks like I was hitting them in my sleep. Everything is happening in slow motion. It takes me a long time to get out of bed. It takes me a long time to clean my room. Collins even yells at me to get a move on. It's not a great start to the day.

I avoided Wired while I was at that writing thing yesterday. But I can't ignore him now. I have to find a way to help him study for our History exam.

Usually I like history. It's stuff that's already happened. It's done. The past can't be changed. So you know exactly what it is — even if you wish with every fibre of your being that you could change that *one* moment. It's not like a video game where you get a do-over or a restart. And the people you take out during the game, that's for real.

The fact that some things don't change is also tricky. Like, my dad's still living in the same spot where the car thing went down. That's why I don't want to get out of here. How am I supposed to go back to the place where it all happened? Sometimes I think it would be easier if my dad moved to a new province, or even a new country. A fresh start for both of us.

But that would be in the future.

And the future scares the hell out of me.

After two and a half years of everything

48

being constant and controlled, I don't know how I would handle anything new or different. Out there, too much can happen. Too much can go wrong. Like it did that day. Like it did for Strummer.

No, staying in is the right thing for me.

✳✳✳

On my way to supper, two Diablos come up behind me and push me to the ground. One dude places his foot on my stomach. "Oh, sorry. Didn't see you there," he says. They both crack up laughing and head toward the cafeteria. Wired reaches me and puts out his hand to pull me up off the floor.

"This will cost you," he says, smirking.

"FINE," I say. "I'll meet you in five." I have to ask a CO to grant me access to the money I earn cleaning the gym so I can get $50. He also lets me into my room to grab the History text. Then I head to dinner.

"Here's the cash." I cringe as I hand Wired the bills. It's money I'll never see again. If Wired repays me in any way, it will be with product, not cash. And I'm not interested in that crap.

We load our plates and grab our seats. I pull out the History text. I figure with food around, Wired will be a captive audience.

"So," I say. "How about I ask you a question and you give me the answer?" I cut into a piece of turkey loaf. "This will test how much you retained from the last time we had our class."

"How about we don't," replies Wired. "I can tell you right now that I don't remember any of the crap we already covered. How about we talk about my future, instead?"

"What do you mean?" I ask.

"Now that I have money, I need a fresh way to move the goods. They're watching me too closely. When I got caught last time, they said next time it won't just be a loss of privileges."

"So don't do it."

"You think it's that easy? I have customers. They're waiting. Besides, you know how crappy it's been this week with the dudes staring you down? If I can't make them happy, they go after both of us. Trust me, we don't want that to happen."

I peer around the room and see that guys from the gang are watching us. I can see the change in Wired's mood. He usually jolts his body all over the place. But now the movements are jerky and more panicked. He's right. We would both be in deep.

"Look, I'll think about it," I tell him. "But don't expect much. I may not want out of here, but I don't want to make a career out of bad choices."

Wired laughs. "Good luck with that!"

I flip the pages of our History text. I can't study right now. And Wired doesn't seem into it, either. Lifting a forkful of mashed potatoes to my mouth, I make small talk. "So you're always going on about getting out of here. When that happens, what's the first thing you're going to do?"

"Get behind the wheel of my Mazda 3." He turns his hands as though he is driving. "Dad got it for me just before I was sent to juvie. He figured it would be an incentive to get out."

"The only car I drove, I crashed . . ." I don't know what just happened. I never talk to anyone, except for my PO, about that day. But Wired doesn't press me. That's one thing I like about him. He never asks questions. He mostly just talks about himself.

"When you're out, you'll get a car," he says. "You'll put a new spin on driving. It'll be good. You'll see."

"I don't plan on getting out. I'm helping you with studying. But like I told you before, don't say anything around Jackson. I don't need him thinking I'm doing a good deed. I don't want early parole. I want to finish every part of my sentence."

"What the hell is your problem, Strider? This isn't where you belong. Or haven't you figured that out yet?"

I feel my face flush and my hands curl into fists. "What you mean is that *you* don't think you belong here. But you haven't changed. In here, you pull the same crap you did out there. It's no different."

This time Wired doesn't blow back at me. He pulls the History text closer. He thumbs through the pages.

"Two things," he says in a controlled voice. "One, I have to pass this test if I want to get my diploma. Two, I have to make it *look* like I'm reformed. That's the only way I'm going to get out of here. This place is killing me." He shakes his head.

In the year I've known Wired, this is the first time he has shared something real. It throws me off. "Okay," I say. "Back to the books. Let's get working."

We finish eating and then study for a few

minutes. The new teacher, Mr. Roberts, comes to see if we need any help. He's here to get to know us better before he comes in to teach our classes. Mr. Roberts's long black hair is parted down the centre. He's wearing a suede vest over a long-sleeved black shirt. His sleeves are rolled up, showing off his eagle tattoo.

"How are you two getting along with History?" he asks.

"We're not," answers Wired.

"Why can't we just write an essay about World War II?" I ask. "How it affects us today? That kind of stuff?"

"Essay questions will be on the test too. Let's check out what you both know so far."

We end up losing an hour of time, relaying facts and getting corrected when we give the wrong answers. Finally Wired has had enough.

As Wired leaves, Roberts leans in. "Okay. I know I just met you. But I believe you're capable of more than the display I saw just now. What's going on?"

"Nothing. I'm just tired. Maybe out there, I'd be able to fly through the coursework. But in here, I have too much on my mind. It's hard to focus on my studies."

"Is there anything I can do to help?"

"Not really. I'll figure it out. I'll study harder. For real." I leave the cafeteria and head to my room before lights-out.

Chapter 7

A New Face

It's Saturday. Wired is bouncing all over the place because he can finally have visitors again. While flipping around at breakfast, he tells me his sister is coming for the first time. My dad is coming to see me too. So, as usual, my energy is low.

Before the visit with my dad, I have to meet with Jackson. It seems the last few days of classes, I haven't been pulling my weight. Trying to do poorly on purpose is harder than I expected. But I've been working at it. I plan to tell Jackson he can take early parole and shelve it. It's just not going to happen.

When I meet Jackson in the visitors' area, he's got a sour face and his arms are crossed. He hasn't even brought any snacks. I feel a rumble in my stomach. Not because I'm hungry but because I suddenly feel anxious. Maybe he isn't taking the news too well. I wish I had a plan B ready.

"Hey, dude." I lay the charm on thick and hope he buys it.

"Sit." He gestures to the chair across the table from him.

As I plant my butt on the seat he lays into me. "What are you doing? Are you failing on purpose? I don't get it, Kevin. You're a good kid. A good kid who made a stupid choice that caused you and others a lot of pain. But you've taken everything we've pushed at you. You've been in here for two and a half years. How long do you figure you should be punished?"

"I dunno," I shrug.

"I believe you can work this out. You can have a good life where you make better choices. But being in here isn't good for you. The longer you stay in, the more worried I get. Settle into your studies so you can pass the tests. Graduating high school should be all that's on your mind right now."

That and *staying in*. To keep him happy, I say, "Fine. I'll work harder. I am helping Wired."

"I heard. That's good. That will also help you to get on the probation board's good side. Keep it up. How is the creative writing going? Did you finish the song you and Strummer were working on before he left?"

"I haven't done much lately. But I will. I want to have something ready for the next session."

"Good," says Jackson, standing. "Planning for the future is what it's all about. The writing class is a step in the right direction. Have a good visit with your dad. And keep your head up!"

We go out our separate doors. Jackson heads back to the world outside. I head back inside, to the gym, to sweep and mop. Afterwards, I shower and head to the visitors' area for the second time today. I'm not sure how my dad will be with me, since I pissed him off on our last visit.

As I enter the room, I spot a girl sitting at one of the other tables. There are two problems right away. One, she has long legs and gives off a cool vibe as she twists one of her blonde braids. She looks my way and our eyes lock. In any other place, that wouldn't be a problem, but we aren't in any other place. Which leads to problem number two, I'm in here and she's out there. Her blue eyes keep holding my gaze. I try a limp smile because I know this can't go anywhere.

When I break eye contact with her, I look up to see Wired scowling at me. There's problem number three. She must be his sister, Larkyn. Larkyn with a backwards *k*. That's how he says she spells her name. I put my head down so Wired won't give me attitude when our visits are over.

Dad opens the door and comes into the room. I point him to an empty table by the vending machine.

As Dad plops down in his seat, I sneak a glance at Larkyn. She's still looking my way. Wired sits down and puts his hand over hers and she turns her gaze from me back to him. The guard lurches toward their table, so Wired slides his hand back into his lap. Dad does his usual hand-wringing motions while waiting for our silence to begin.

I am so focused on Larkyn I forget to be stressed about being with Dad.

"Well," he starts. "I'm here. I'm on time. Anything you want to say about that?" There is an edge to his voice.

I deserve it.

Larkyn sneaks a sideways grin at me. I grin back. "No, I'm good." I say out loud.

Dad gets up and heads over to the vending machine. "Coke?" he asks.

I nod. Dad returns to his seat and slides the can my way. He's bought a root beer for himself and he throws a bag of red liquorice on the table after tearing open the package. He bites into one. I remember how we used to love watching movies and chewing on liquorice. That was back when I was young and Mom was still in the picture. I feel a little raw, remembering a nice scene with my dad.

"Thanks," I mumble.

"Sure," Dad says. "Listen, last time I was here I didn't get to finish telling you that thing I figured out." He looks up at me, like he's expecting me to blow up again.

I sit quietly, waiting to hear what he has to say.

He takes a deep breath. "When I was walking Gemini, he was tugging on his leash.

I mean, tugging hard. He misses being able to run with you." He pauses. I stay chill and Dad continues. "It made me think of you and me. We're kind of leashed up too. Tied up . . . tied together. Oh, crap. That's not what I mean. What I am trying to say is . . . this isn't making any sense, is it?"

I shrug my shoulders.

"The past. Everything that happened. It's where you and I are stuck. We're both stuck *back then*. Like we're tied to that *one day*. Like a leash, that's holding us back."

Before I can respond, Dad shakes his head. He takes a long swig of his drink. "Just forget it. It made sense at the time."

I run his words through my head. Dad and I *are* tied to the past. I guess that's like being leashed up, or tied to one memory. We always end up back there, at that one day. At the exact same thing. It ends up in the same place every time. I don't know if we can break free.

But Dad is trying to sort things out.

That is something. So I nod, and Dad seems satisfied. That is as good as it will get. For now.

Larkyn stands up and my eyes are drawn to her again. She's wearing pink and blue leggings and a matching top. They cling to her curves. She turns and smiles at me as she leaves the room. Wired heads out of the visitors' area.

The CO calls, "Time."

Dad stands. As he begins to head for the door I say, "Thanks for coming."

I can't see the expression on his face, but I see him nod his head. I head back to my room.

I pull out my chair at the desk and plop down. I look up at Weed. "Do spiders have mates?" I ask her. "I mean, I've never seen another spider in here. Ever since I've been in, I've convinced myself the only thing I miss is my dog, Gemini. But the way I feel right now, I guess I miss having a chance to be with people. To hang out at the beach. To chill with friends. Or to be with a girl. A girl like Larkyn. Know what I mean?"

Weed doesn't answer me. But as though she knows I am in deep, she slides down a thread of silk and hangs above my head.

Chapter 8

Future and Past

Since the writers will be coming soon, I work on Strummer's song. I am surprised to find that Larkyn is on my mind constantly. I wish I had asked Tanika out, but I'm pretty sure I could never have a future with her. Not now. Not after everything that has happened. But Larkyn would "get" me. She would understand, since she has a brother inside. Every time I looked her way the other day, she was smiling at me. That's got to say something.

I'm pretty sure we connected, even if it was only in glances.

Leaving juvie has never been on my radar. It scares the hell out of me. But for the last few days, I find myself thinking about it in my free time. How Gemini and I could run on the beach like we used to, playing with my Frisbee. And I've been thinking about what it would be like to go for coffee with a girl. To have someone pretty sitting across from me, smiling and laughing at what I say. What if that could happen? Larkyn is cool. But she's out and I'm in.

I tap my desk like it's a Taiko drum. I beat out a rhythm and imagine Larkyn grooving to my tune. A line for a song comes to me: *The ocean in your eyes and the future in your smile.* That might work. The next line comes: *The distance is far but I'd walk every mile.* Okay, skip that line.

But it does make me think. The distance between me and being with any girl isn't measured in miles or kilometres. It's different. After everything that's happened, could I really walk that distance? It would mean agreeing to early parole. It would mean doing the stuff that Jackson asks of me. These thoughts roll around my head for most of the day.

After classes, I walk to the visitors' area. Jackson wants to meet with me again. For once, he has good timing. On the way, I decide I'll ask him if Larkyn can be added to my visitor list. I figure it won't take long to get her approved because she's already been vetted for Wired. Of course, while we were in class, Wired told me to leave his sister alone. He saw us exchange looks and doesn't want it to go anywhere. Like he can sit in judgment.

"Hey," I say to Jackson. I park myself across from him. Today, he's wearing khaki colours and I'm in all white.

"How's it going?" he asks as he gulps his soda. That's a good sign. He's back to getting us pop and snacks.

"Pretty good," I reply. And I mean it. I feel more hopeful than I have in two and half years.

But in seconds that good feeling disappears.

"Kevin," Jackson says, "Do you remember me mentioning a new visitor? One that may come to see you? Well, she did all the steps she needed to. And we fast-tracked her approval. She'd like to come see you this weekend. What do you think?"

"I guess that depends on who she is." It freaks me out that both times Jackson has mentioned this visitor, he's left out the most important part — who she is. Could it be my mom? What would I say to her after all these years?

"Before I say her name I want you to really think about meeting with her. How it could help your early probation."

In my head I wonder how seeing anyone could help me get out of here early. Then Jackson says his next words and my world implodes.

"Her name is Aisha. She's the daughter of the man you harmed."

I hear a buzzing sound. Just like I did that day. My heart has jumped into my throat and I feel like I'm choking. *Why her? Why now? What does she want from me?*

I must have said the words out loud. Jackson answers me. "She wants to meet you so she can ask you questions about what you were thinking that day. She wants to know how you feel about what happened. I believe she wants to move forward. And she thinks you can help her to do that."

My words roll out fast. "How can I help her? I have enough trouble getting through each day myself. How do I tell her I *wasn't* thinking that day? That's why this happened. I just jumped in the car. Then I thought I was being followed by the cops. I hit a sheet of ice. I slid. What can I say that will make a difference?"

"You'd be surprised. She never got to meet you. I feel you can move forward. And she wants to move forward too. But that means talking to each other."

I'm shaking as though the air conditioning has come on and is blasting down my neck. I'm freaked out about this girl named Aisha. And like that time when my dad left the hose running in the backyard, suddenly my memories are spilling out like fast-running water. Water that freezes when it hits the cold air.

I feel as though I am behind the wheel of the car again.

I can feel the slip of tires on the icy surface. Screams mingle with the crunch of the car as it hits the pole. A red-hot pain sears into my brain. It's like I am reliving my daily nightmare, only the images are ten times stronger.

Then I feel a hand on my arm. Someone is trying to talk to me.

"Kevin . . . Kevin. What's up? What just happened?" Jackson is holding both my arms.

His face is inches from mine. "Are you okay?"

"Yeah," I say. I jerk away from him. He drops his arms. "I just had a flash."

"Of the day of the accident?"

"Don't call it that."

"What, an accident?"

"Yeah. We both know that isn't true." My head bows down. I am having trouble looking at my PO. How could I possibly sit across from the daughter of the man I hurt? How would I be able to look her in the eyes? Especially as they well up with tears. Not going to happen. Remorse fills me and hardens like concrete. It's heavy and weighs me down.

"Kevin," Jackson breaks into my thoughts again. "Taking the car was no accident. You're right. It was reckless and stupid. It was an impulsive move. You didn't think about the consequences. But sliding on the ice . . ."

"Happened because I was going too fast for the road conditions. I was trying to ditch the cop car. It probably wasn't even after me.

In fact, I'm sure that's what the cop said. He wasn't chasing me and didn't know the car was stolen. But I panicked."

"Okay, Kevin, but life goes on. You don't know what Aisha is thinking *now*. Consider meeting with her."

"I don't think I can. I wouldn't know what to say. Look, I just met Wired's sister, Larkyn. I'm having enough trouble thinking about what I would say to her if we got to hang out. Aisha would be too much pressure."

Jackson asks the question I can't. "Are you hoping to have a visit with Larkyn? I don't know if that's a good idea. She and Wired . . . that's a problem waiting to happen. Aisha is a step forward. You won't get anywhere meeting with Larkyn."

Now I feel a hot flush run into my cheeks. I stand and lean toward Jackson. "Larkyn made me think about getting out — made me think about it for the FIRST time. That's something. But, Aisha, that makes me want to stay in here.

That's too much to ask right now."

"Then how about this," Jackson offers. "I think about helping you to see Larkyn. And you think about meeting with Aisha."

I turn toward the door that takes me back inside. "Fine."

I am not fine with seeing Aisha. But now it seems even more important that I meet Larkyn. She could be someone I could talk to about all of this. Her smile alone would help me deal with this crap. And she'd be better to talk to than my spider.

Chapter 9

Good News

It's been two days since I met with Jackson. I grab my food tray and load it with cereal and a glass of milk. The milk sloshes all over the tray on my way to the table. I sit away from everyone. I've been doing that for days. I avoid any of the guys, especially Wired. But today, Wired is sitting three tables over, waving his arms at me. I ignore him. Out of the corner of my eye, I can see him making an idiot of himself trying to get my attention.

I guess his coming to my table is out of the question. The shuffle to Wired's table is slow. But when I get there, I lay into him. "What the hell is your problem?"

"I talked with my sister on the phone last night. She said she's been approved to visit with you. *Today*!" He says it like it's the worst thing in the world.

"I don't get it," I say. "Jackson didn't say anything to me."

"Maybe he will when you see him."

"I guess. But wait . . . why do you know this before me?" The news I might get to actually meet Larkyn is sinking in. I'm suddenly overheating.

Wired is glaring at me but doesn't answer.

"I'll check with Jackson," I tell him. "I'm meeting with him in a few hours. Maybe he'll tell me then."

Wired puts his face inches from mine. "And that's when you say *NO*."

"Like hell," I shove him away from me.

"You don't tell me how to run my life. Just a few weeks ago you were the one crying because you had no visitors. Who do I have coming to see me? My dad. Oh, and it's always a great visit." My volume has increased with the tension in my body. "If I can talk with your sister . . . it will definitely be better than hanging around the losers in here. If Jackson says she's approved, then I'll say *thanks*. That's it. Got it?" I've moved within inches of his face.

Wired backs up and his fist pounds the table. "She's with me first. We'll see what happens after that." He marches to a table with some of the dudes who have muscle.

I know it's designed to intimidate me, so I ignore him. Even so, a stare from one of the big dudes gets under my skin.

I regret giving Wired crap minutes after our blow-up. If I am able to see his sister, I don't want him giving her the wrong idea about me. He can make it so she won't want to visit. And I don't need the Diablos after me. I give my head a shake.

All the way through my chores I check over my shoulder every few minutes. I feel as though I'm being watched. I will see Larkyn-with-a-backwards-*k*. But I better work something out with Wired before I get in too deep. Maybe I should give him some more cash?

But the scene with Wired gets under my skin. Does he figure his sister deserves someone better than me? What the hell! I saw the way she was looking at me. These thoughts play back and forth in my head as the morning goes on.

After my chores, I get cleaned up, in case I am given permission to see Larkyn. My CO supervises while I shave with the kit I just bought. Some days having someone watch every move I make really gets on my nerves. And today especially, I wish I could wear my own clothes. To give Larkyn a sense of my style. But I pull on the same sweats as everyone else. Mine are too baggy.

After I shower, I gel the top part of my light brown hair so it stands up. This gives me more height. I noticed when Larkyn visited Wired that she is tall.

I'm too nervous to eat lunch. So I just wait to hear if I have good news from Jackson. He doesn't come to visit me like I expected. Instead, he calls.

"Hey, Kevin," I hear over the phone. "I still don't think it is a good plan, but I have approved your visit with Larkyn. Just be cautious. But I do like that you are thinking of your future now. And if this helps get you on track, I'm willing to help make it happen."

I sense real worry in his voice. "Okay," I say. "But the visit will be good, you'll see."

"I hope so. Now, the second reason I called is to check in about Aisha. What are your thoughts about seeing her?"

Of course, Jackson has to kill the moment

by bringing up Aisha. I feel a tremor run down my legs. "Okay, I will see her. But not today."

"No, of course not. I'll book her for Saturday."

Jackson hangs up. While I am excited about seeing Larkyn, panic rises in my throat. It sits right under my Adam's apple, making it hard to swallow or breathe. I head to my room. I lie back on my bed and try to chill. I never asked Tanika out when we were in school. Now I wish I had. I wish I had more experience with girls and knew what the hell to say to Larkyn. And I wish I didn't have the thought of Aisha's visit looming in the back of my mind.

The idea of seeing Aisha keeps creeping into my thoughts. And every time that happens, I feel like I am back at the scene of the crime. Back in the frosty air of that wintry morning. Now two things are at war in my brain. If I let myself think about getting out, I can hang with Larkyn. But then, how would I face Aisha? If I see her, it will open the floodgates to how I feel about what happened. I don't know if I can handle that.

The afternoon crawls and I'm stuck in my head. It seems like forever before my CO calls me to the visitors' area. I run my fingers through my hair and adjust my sweat pants so they're sitting on my hips. Not much else I can do to look any better. And I push any thoughts of Aisha out of the way so I can focus on Larkyn.

Wired is nowhere to be seen as I head down the hall.

Chapter 10

First Meeting

Larkyn is already at a table when I arrive. She has a ginger ale in her hand and nods as I come in. I don't know how to greet her, so I just say "hi" and plop down in the chair across from her. The table between us seems as big as a canyon. I wish there was nothing between me and Larkyn right now but air. And not too much of that, either.

"Hey," Larkyn says.

Her voice is silky. I exhale the breath I've been holding. There is a moment of silence and

I don't know how to fill it. Now that she's in front of me, it's hard to talk. I blurt out, "So you saw your brother today?" Maybe I'll find out what he told her about us.

"Yeah. It's been tough seeing Weston these past two visits."

Right, Wired's real name is Weston.

"He's been in a long time," she says. "And I had to go through hell to get in here. Some fat dude searched me, and I had to empty my pockets. Then I got crotch-sniffed by a dog."

"Crap," I say. Maybe seeing me isn't worth the trouble. "I hope you don't have to go through that when you visit me next time."

"Already thinking we'll have a next time?" She raises her eyebrow.

"Maybe . . . yeah?" I shrug my shoulders as I breathe in her perfume. It's kind of earthy, like soft musk.

"You know my brother doesn't like us hanging out."

"I don't know what Wired's problem is.

You and I haven't even gotten to know each other. Why is he so against us meeting?"

"He's always been protective of me. He thinks he knows what's best. But don't worry. I make up my own mind about things."

I feel heat flush into my cheeks. What if she makes up her mind that I'm not interesting? But I nod. "Good thing to know. I made up my mind too. Even against your brother's wishes, I asked to meet you."

"I like hearing that."

She puts her hands in front of mine. I should take her hand. Instead, I stare at her black nails so I can keep some sense of control.

"So how are you doing in here?" Larkyn asks. "I can't imagine spending one day in this place. Weston says you came in at fifteen. That's younger than he was when he got sentenced."

"Yeah, it's been hard. This place is hard." That's why her softness feels right. It lightens the air. She brings warmth to the cold routine of doing time.

Silence again.

"So," she says, "What do you like to do? I mean, what did you like to do . . . before . . ." She looks down at the can of ginger ale in her hand. I didn't want this to be awkward, but how can it not be? I'm *in* and she's *out*. She looks younger than me, but I bet she's experienced way more than I have. My life stopped at fifteen. Hers didn't.

I change the focus to Larkyn. "Are you taking driving lessons?" At sixteen you can get your learner's permit in BC. Unless you're behind bars. Like me.

"Yeah. I do two days a week, after school."

"Vancouver streets are pretty busy. How's it going?"

"I freak out at least once every drive. Plus, there are two classmates with me and we trade off. So I have others watching and judging me. That part sucks."

"I know all about being judged."

"Sorry," she replies. She slides her hand even closer to mine.

Our fingers are almost touching. I look at the CO on duty. He's looking the other way, watching one of the Diablos with his girlfriend. I wouldn't normally go this fast with someone I just met. But who knows if we'll have another chance to hang out. I let my fingers slide over hers. Her warm hands send a tingling feeling into my fingers that runs up my arms.

"Enough," says the CO. Damn, he must have eyes in the back of his head.

My hand slides down to my side. Larkyn's cheeks flush.

If this were a real first meeting, a real date, we wouldn't have some guard telling us how close we can sit. Or whether or not we can link our fingers together. Larkyn looks around the room. I can sense she's embarrassed. If I want to see her again, I need to figure out how to save this moment.

"So what about you?" I say, holding her gaze. I don't want to lose the connection we just made. "What do you like to do, after school? For fun?" As soon as I ask, it seems like a strange question. But the idea that Larkyn can choose what she wants to do makes me think about what I used to like to do in my free time. When I had choices.

"I'm working part-time at a movie theatre. It sucks. I think the manager hired me for one reason, and it has nothing to do with selling popcorn."

I cringe. "Tell the jerk to keep his hands off . . ."

"Believe me, I'm doing everything I can to stay out of his way. He's slimy, and rude to most of the staff. Great first job, hey?"

"And what about school?"

"I'm in grade eleven. Almost final exam time."

I shake my head. I've been blowing off the coursework because I don't want early parole. Sitting across from Larkyn, I'm starting to rethink things.

She goes on, "My parents harp on me daily

about not turning out like my brother. What do they know?"

"Yeah. Parents!" It's weird thinking about someone else's family. I've avoided that line of thought ever since the day that got me thrown in here. Now I suddenly recall my mom and dad back when we still lived together.

I used to think my parents got along pretty well. I ignored the signs that things were busting up. Like my dad staying out late and not coming home to dinner. A few nights, he wasn't home when I got up in the morning. One day, I came back from a volleyball game and my parents were screaming at each other. Then Mom bounced.

She left through the front door and didn't come back.

Ever.

When I look up, Larkyn is studying me. I pull a comment from the thickness of the moment. "My dad . . . well . . . he and I never talk. We're kind of stuck in this cycle of silence.

Sometimes I think it's better that way. Other stuff is too hard to talk about. You know what I mean?"

"And your mom?"

"We don't see each other. I mean, she hasn't been around . . ."

"I'm sorry." Larkyn has a warmth in her eyes I could get lost in. For a long time. It's like I forget where I am.

Larkyn changes the subject and we end up talking like we've known each other forever. The next fifteen minutes fly by. Twice, I laugh. And that's a big deal.

Then I hear the words. "Time," the CO tells us that our visit is over.

A shuffle of feet rings through the room as visitors stand and prepare to leave. Larkyn rushes to my side of the table and gives me a hug.

Then she's gone.

Chapter 11

Trigger

Still reeling from my visit with Larkyn, I feel the rest of the week go by quickly. Wired gives me crap daily about seeing Larkyn. I take it. I figure it's better to make him think I'm not going to see his sister again. That way he won't make my life even more of a living hell in between visits. I also bribe him with more cash to keep both him and the other dudes off my back.

But I'm not seeing Larkyn today. Instead, I'm getting ready for the visit with Aisha.

When I woke up this morning, I was shaking. The court trial was vivid in my mind. The feel of the chairs, how they were cold and hard. The air in the room lacked oxygen. I remember how my temples pinched with stress. I spent a lot of time looking at my hands in my lap on the day of sentencing. I couldn't look at the man's wife. During the hearing, I learned about the son and daughter. How they were just a bit older than me. They didn't attend. I remember their mom saying it would be too much for them.

Hell, it was too much for me. But I had to be there. I had to face the consequences of my actions. I had no choice.

And today, my heart feels like lead. How have I been able to block out this feeling for so long? I know I've been scared about life on the outside. But maybe something else has been keeping me here. Maybe I am afraid of facing Aisha. I'm afraid of facing the man's family because of what I did.

Two and a half years ago, Aisha was in grade

twelve. I guess that would make her twenty, or twenty-one now? She would have gone to my school. I never got my yearbook when I was in grade ten, since I didn't finish the school year. And now she'll be in university, or working. I hope. I hope she got on with her life. I hope she hasn't been stuck in the past, like me.

I shake off the memory and get cleaned up before the visit. But it doesn't feel anything like it did when I was going to meet Larkyn. As I put my arms into the sleeves of my green sweatshirt and pull it over my head, I feel dizzy. I have to sit on the edge of my bed to get my bearings. The room is swaying. It closes in on me. I consider calling Jackson to cancel the visit. But ever since I met with Larkyn, I've been putting an effort into studying. Jackson thinks meeting with Aisha will help my early parole. So I want to do what I can to make that happen. In case I can get it together and be ready for a life beyond this shit hole.

But I'm scared.

I'm afraid of seeing the pain in this

woman's face. The pain I put there.

I shave while Collins keeps watch. I find myself looking at him in between draws of the blade along my cheek. What does he really think of us? All of us in here. As I ask myself that question, the blade catches my flesh. Blood trickles down my chin. Red.

A red scarf on white snow.

All of a sudden, my guilt erupts like a volcano spewing hot lava down the mountainside. Red hot lava. Burning everything in its wake. Once a volcano pops, you can't put a stopper in it. You can't push all the hot lava back into the volcano. It just seeps into everything. Like my guilt. Suddenly, it's flowing around me. I can't push it back down.

I can't block these feelings any longer.

"Look, Collins," I gasp. "I need to call Jackson. NOW! I am NOT doing this visit. He can ban me from Larkyn, the writing group, whatever he wants. I am not ready for this. GET IT?"

Collins shakes his head. "Not happening, man. It's time for your visit right now. Your visitor is already here. You've got to face this."

"But how . . ."

Collins points to my chin. The blood has stopped trickling but I have a red streak down my face. I dab at it with a tissue. Collins holds the door open. He gestures for me to follow him. After what seems like several minutes I finally find the courage to follow my CO down the hall.

My walk toward the visiting area is slow. There isn't any spring in my step. Instead, I can barely make my legs move forward. Earlier, when I told Jackson I didn't know what to say to Aisha, he told me to just listen. Let her talk. Let her guide the discussion.

So that's what I plan to do. If I can ever make it into the room.

Just before I get to the door, I can see through the window into the visitors' area. There are four tables with people waiting at them. One is a family of three. At the next table is a young dude, close to my age. The next two tables each have a woman at them. But I know which one is Aisha immediately. She's looking straight into my eyes. She's looking to see if I care about what happened.

I want to bolt. I don't want to face her. But now that she has spotted me, leaving might give her the wrong idea. I don't want to hurt her more. So I take a deep breath and open the door. My chest heaves as I try to swallow too much air, too fast. When I reach her table, I don't know what to do. So I just stand there. She motions for me to sit down.

She's trembling. As I sit, I can feel the table jiggle from her legs bouncing and knocking into it. "I'm Aisha," she says. "I, uh, wanted this to be different. This isn't how I meant for us to meet. I . . . today . . ."

She doesn't finish the sentence. A bead of sweat rolls down the side of her face. She tugs at her hijab and wipes away the moisture. I haven't looked directly into her eyes. That is too much. That's too intense. But her nerves shake me up. We're both struggling.

Aisha begins speaking again. "I had a terrible time getting here. At a four-way stop sign, this idiot blew through the intersection. He acted like I was the only one who had to pay attention to the signs. I was already rattled because of our visit. Now, I can't shake this feeling. He nearly smashed my car. I . . ." Her eyes are darting everywhere. She scans the room like she's in danger.

Someone almost hit her on the way here. A car. A near accident.

Now I'm sweating. My pulse rips up inside me. I stand up. My hand grabs the table so I can keep my balance. I'm not ready for this. Not now. Not with what she just said.

"Wait, please," she pleads. "Don't go."

I sit back down. But now it's my leg bouncing triple beats.

"I just want to ask . . . I mean, I just want to know if . . ."

I'm sorry. That's what she needs to hear.

That's what she wants to know. I think of
an old Elton John song. He only got it half
right — sorry isn't just the hardest word. It's
a lame word. It's a non-word. It doesn't mean
anything. It doesn't carry weight or take up
space. Right now as I need to say it, I know the
word isn't big enough to fill this room. It isn't
big enough to erase what happened to her dad.

It's just not enough.

I look up to see Aisha staring at me. My
eyes are moist. Hers are wet pools and tears
begin to flow down her cheeks.

"I'm sorry," I say. But I don't say the word
to apologize for what happened two and a half
years ago. I say it over my shoulder, because I'm
bolting for the door. I say it because I can't do
this. This was a stupid idea. I don't know what
the hell Jackson was thinking by putting us
together in a room. How can that fix anything?

Chapter 12

Lockdown

I leave Aisha sitting at the table by herself. I fly into the hallway. I don't go to my room but stop and pace the halls. Back and forth for six trips. My fists clench harder with each round. My breath is shallower with every step. I bite my lip and shake my head. I'm going to explode.

A hand touches my shoulder. Thinking it is Wired, I turn and shove the person.

Through the fire of my emotions, I see that it's my CO. Crap!

He must have spotted me and thought I was escalating. He's right. I offer my hand to help him up. But he's already half-standing.

"You know the drill," he states.

I turn so Collins can restrain my arms behind my back. He walks me to my room and as my door slams shut I hear him say into his walkie-talkie, "Lockdown on level four."

Great. Not only did I royally screw up the visit with Aisha, now I have earned my entire ward a lockdown. That won't go over well with the guys in my section.

Being on lockdown means you can't leave your room for the allotted time. This time it's two hours. Other than clothes and my school books, I have nothing in my room. Nothing to occupy my time. Now I miss more than ever being allowed to have a cell phone. So I try to bury myself in my studies. Besides, if I'm studying, I don't have to think about the botched visit with Aisha. How I left her sitting there with all her questions.

But Aisha made the effort to come see me. She had the courage to walk through the door and wait at a table for me. Even after almost having her car hit on the way here.

And I bolted.

Jackson will probably revoke my privileges to see Larkyn. What does it matter? I was only fooling myself. How could I think that hanging out with a girl would keep my mind from running the same clip over and over — the scene from that day? It will always be the first thing I think of when I wake up. And now I feel the full impact of it. Of my actions. Of what I did.

Everyone will know it was me who screwed up. So when the lockdown is lifted and our doors open for us to attend the evening program, I don't leave my room. But in seconds, Wired is at my door.

"Wow!" he says. "Knocking down a guard. You've got balls after all."

"And I thought you were here to give me crap."

"I won't need to. The Diablos are pissed. Not just those who got shut down for the past few hours. Everyone is antsy. Guys in here don't like waiting."

"But I gave you extra cash. What's the problem?"

"Like I said before, I'm being watched. And after what happened with you, the COs are being bigger jerks than usual. I need someone . . ."

"No! I told you before. I'm not interested." I don't want to face anyone else. But I don't want to be stuck in this room with Wired hanging at my door. I brush past him and head to the TV room.

Judge Judy is blaring from the screen. It's not like I get to choose what to watch. Macaroni and I never get to choose. If you don't like what's playing, you don't stick around. But today, since the room has only three guys sitting in it, and they aren't gang members, I chill. Escaping here is about the only thing that will get me through the rest of the day.

✱✱✱

Jackson comes to see me a week after the blow-up with Aisha. I sweated every day waiting for him to ream me out. Now that the time is here, I'm relieved. We can get it over with. I can return to the routine I had before all of this started. Even if it means not seeing Larkyn-with-a-backwards-*k*.

"Hey, Kevin," Jackson says. He has our usual arsenal on the table. Peace offering, maybe.

I feel unsure as I answer with, "How's it going?"

"Better for me than you, I hear."

"Yeah, it was a crappy week. Listen, I didn't mean to blow off Aisha like that. She was talking about a car accident she almost had on the way in to visit me. How was I supposed to respond? I mean shit . . ."

"Yeah, she told me. She feels bad about sharing that with you. She realizes that it was a trigger for both of you. She knows that's why you left. She wants to give it another shot. What do you say?"

I look around the room. Visitors everywhere. Lots of people sit casually with their sentenced son. I wonder how we looked last week. It surprises me to hear that Aisha wants to try again. To give me a second chance. I didn't expect that.

I answer Jackson, "I don't know. The whole time I was with Aisha, all I could think about was this stupid word: *sorry*. A word with no meaning. Not to me, anyway."

"You don't think apologizing for what happened will make a difference?"

"How can it? It can't give them back the life they had before I ran into . . ."

"But it can be the first step in building a connection. A real connection. Where you talk. Where you listen. Forgiveness is . . ."

"Not something I'm looking for. I know that now. I know now that is part of what's been keeping me here. I don't deserve to be released."

"Well, Larkyn has also asked to see you. How about we approve Larkyn for now and give you a week or so before trying with Aisha again? Maybe meeting with Larkyn will get you back on track. I know you said she gave you purpose. Let's start there. She's seeing Wired this afternoon. I could pull some strings."

"I can think about it. But I can't guarantee that I'll be ready for a round two with Aisha."

"Fair enough. I'll see about extending Larkyn's time to give you a chance to chat today."

It's so pathetic, it's almost funny. My PO is agreeing to something he believes isn't in my best interest.

I leave the room and wait. I wait for Jackson to work some magic. I wait to hear that I can see Larkyn. I wonder if seeing her will get me out of my head.

Chapter 13

Scammed

My CO finds me in the hall to tell me the visit has been approved. Collins says I am to be escorted to the visitors' area. My pits are sweating as I pass through the door.

Larkyn is sitting at the same table as last time. Her smile lights up the room as I head toward her.

"I hope it was easier to get in here this time," I say. "No jerks messing with you?"

"Still got patted down. Still emptied my

pockets and had to endure the dog. Maybe if I just come to see *you*, they'll drop one thing each time. Eventually, maybe I'll just be down to basics."

"Whatever that is." It makes me think of my dad. I never pay attention to what he has to go through to get in here to see me. Out loud I say, "Good thing you passed the tests. I overheard one of the guys saying that a dude in prison had his mom visit. The drug-scanning tester they use there gave her a false positive so they didn't let her in. His mom!"

"Seriously?"

"Yeah." I shake my head and move my chair around to the side of the table, closer to her.

"Weston says that if anything like that happens here, they suspend your privileges. Then that person may not get to visit again. With Weston, I'll still have to go through the whole thing each time. They watch him really closely."

"Better than prison where you may be stuck with glass between you, even just to talk. What a way to visit. I'm glad we can sit close, like this." Aisha and the accident are being pushed to the back of my thoughts. I inch forward. Larkyn leans in.

I act on a sudden urge. I pull her face up to mine so we can kiss. Just as I suspected, her lips are soft and moist. My body stirs.

"That's enough!" My CO steps closer to our table. We pull apart.

Larkyn rubs the back of her hand across her lips. Agony!

Collins doesn't drop his gaze, making sure Larkyn and I don't try to get close again. If I show him my hands are busy, maybe he'll leave us alone. So I take Larkyn's empty coffee cup, the one she got from the machine, and wipe the inside of it with my hand. I don't want coffee stains on my sweat pants. It's white day again. Then I turn the cup upside down and hold it between my knees. The heavy paper bottom acts like the surface of a drum. I start playing it with my fingers.

"That's cool. You're good," says Larkyn, bopping her head to the rhythm. "Oh, I can't believe I didn't ask you this question last time. Weston calls you Strider. I never thought about it just being a name you use in here. Like how you call him Wired. What's your real name?"

"Kevin." Again I feel strange saying a name I've used all my life except for in here. It seems foreign.

"Kevin. But I like Strider too. That's a chill name."

"Not as chill as Larkyn-with-a-backwards-*k*."

Larkyn smiles. "So I hear it's almost your birthday? Won't you be one year closer to being legal to drink?"

"Makes no difference to me. I'm stuck in here, either way." I continue drumming on the upside-down paper cup, but the tempo has increased.

"True." She leans in and lowers her voice.

"But I bet you *could* get something if you wanted it." She raises an eyebrow. "You know, to celebrate."

"Yeah, your brother . . . Forget it." I don't want to go down that road. I don't want to talk about Wired and his plans. I don't want her mixed up in any of that. "When's your birthday?"

"My birthday is in September. But if your birthday is coming up, that makes you a Gemini. You're kind of like two people."

I chuckle. "That's why I named my dog Gemini. He's a Husky with one blue eye and one brown eye. Like there are two dogs inside him."

"You must miss him," she says. "But you being a Gemini is a good thing for being stuck in this place. You can be the guy who does time, and you can be the guy you were before — the guy you'll be again when you get out." She grins.

The guy I'll be again. I repeat the words in my head. Somehow I don't think that's possible. Not after everything. There was a before, but after looks very different.

Larkyn studies me. Then she blurts out, "Shoot! This is harder than I thought it would be. I didn't count on liking you."

Her words pull me out of my head. "What does that mean?"

"I'm into you. I wasn't expecting that. And not so fast." She sighs and looks around the room. Our time is almost up. She leans in close. I think it's because she wants to kiss me again. But I read things all wrong. Her reason for leaning in is as far from wanting to kiss me as you can get.

She whispers, "So my brother thinks I can get stuff in, the next time I come. They're watching me when I visit him. But if I just come to see you, I don't think it'll be as tough. Maybe on the next visit, or the visit after, I can move some stuff through you. What do you think?"

I stand up so fast the coffee cup tumbles to the floor. My knees knock into the table, right on that sharp spot where it shoots pain to the back of your eyeballs. I press my hand against my head and stagger backwards like I've been hit by a huge wind. "What do I think?!" I say, my voice in all caps. "Are you crazy?!" I look around to see if Wired is smirking from some other table. Or if the Diablos have been waiting for my answer. But it's just a couple of dudes and their families. And of course, two COs. Did they hear what she just asked me?

My words come out in a stutter. "I have to go. I had a song I was working on for you . . . I can't . . . Have a good life . . ." And then I'm out the door.

As I fly down the hall I see Wired on his way to the cafeteria. I run up behind him and grab his sweatshirt. I pull hard. Because I caught him unaware, I'm able to haul him to the ground. I kick his stomach before his arms can come up to protect himself. He curls into a ball, giving me less area to hurt. I'm just about to kick him again when I feel an arm squeeze my throat in a chokehold.

Instantly, I am out of breath. Wired gets up and throws a punch to my gut as the Diablo holds me still. Then two more Diablos arrive. One guy kicks me. Then a ton of fists swing at me before a guard comes into view, shouting at us to stop.

Everyone flees. As the guy holding me lets go, I crumple to the ground. My groin hurts. My head hurts. My arm is all twisted in knots. As I'm escorted to the medical room, I hear a voice over the PA.

"Lockdown on level four."

Again. Second time in a week.

And my fault. Both times.

Chapter 14

Tested

They keep the lockdown all through the night. Muffins and milk cartons are brought to each room for breakfast. When they finally lift the lockdown at lunchtime, I'm escorted from the medical room to a private room, with my lunch.

Jackson is waiting. "What the hell, Kevin?"

"Okay, before you blast me, hear me out. You were right. About everything. You figured out Wired and his sister right away. I was too stupid and too blind to see it. They scammed me. They set me up. The only good thing is that Larkyn didn't plant something on me before I flew out of the visitors' area." I feel steamed all over again. Instead of sitting to eat my lunch, I pace the room. Jackson motions for me to sit down, but I'm too fired up.

"But why pick a fight with Wired?" asks Jackson. "You should know better. He's the most protected guy in here. And now you have the bruises to prove it."

I reach up to my face. I have a cut lip and a welt forming under my eye. My groin still aches and my arm feels like it was twisted in a vice grip.

"Larkyn. She played me. They both did. I thought she really wanted to meet me. That she was into me. But it was all a plan to get contraband in through me. Use Strider. You know, the guy who only ever has *one* visitor. Nobody will be checking things on his watch. Who would come to see him, anyway?"

"Pity really doesn't look good on you. I'm not going to say what I'm thinking. You already figured things out. But I was hoping I was wrong. It's a crappy way to find out that some people will always be players. They're out for themselves and you got caught in the middle."

"Yeah, well, it was good timing. I needed that wake-up call to put me back on track. I don't want to see any visitors — not even my dad. I don't care about early parole. Just let me go back to the way things were. Slow and easy."

"Your dad and Aisha are still important. Don't let what happened with Larkyn ruin your chances for early probation. Right now things look bad. But sort this out and get back on track. Your request might still be accepted by the board."

"It's not my request. It never has been. You seem to think I'm ready. Well, I'm not."

"Hang on," Jackson sighs. "Strummer nicknamed you Strider, right? I thought you said you watched the movies?"

"I did."

"Then how did you miss the biggest part of Strider's character? The fact that he doesn't give up. Everything is against him. Nothing comes easy. He has to work his butt off, but he stays the course. He does the time. And in the end it works out and he gets everything he wants."

"But what about all the shit that happens on the way to getting what he wants?"

"That's called *life*. I'll say it again, Kevin. You're a good kid. You can make this work. Especially if you start believing in yourself the way I do."

Good to know that at least one person is on my side.

✱✱✱

Even though everyone else is off lockdown, I am held in my room for two extra days. Collins says it's for my safety. I've been eating my meals in my room and haven't had any visitors. But since I have to write the History exam, they will be letting me join the others again.

I have lots of time to study. But I don't crack the spine of the book. Not even when Roberts visits me in my room to help me prepare for the test. I rip up the song I was working on for Wired's sister. The only thing I put any effort into finishing is Strummer's song. Strummer never let me down.

Then I knock off some ideas for a song of my own. For the chorus, I capture thoughts about being played. Being stupid.

But I don't get to share my lyrics with Sean, because the writing group is cancelled for today. Everyone else is back in the main space, but I guess they didn't want to chance another incident. So no one gets to enjoy the writing session.

Because of me.

The only good thing about being on lockdown by myself is that my bruises, inside and out, get a bit of time to heal. I think the bruises on the outside are faring better than the other ones.

I saunter down the hall to the classroom where we'll take the exam. I think about what I'll say to Wired. But as I near the door, two Diablos catch up to me.

The big dude talks first. At the sound of his voice, my hand flies toward my throat. He must be the jerk who choked me.

"Wired needs to pass the test today," he says. "And you'll make it happen. Then you *will* meet his sister." He spots Collins coming down the hall. "Oh, and good luck with the exam."

I shake my head and go to the classroom. No one is in the room yet. I grab a spot against the far wall. In seconds, a flurry of movement indicates that others have arrived. I feel a swoosh beside me. Wired slides into the seat. He winks at me and waits for the exams to be handed out. Roberts gives us a pep talk on how he knows we'll all do well. Then he tells us we can turn over the page and begin. We get one hour.

The first part is multiple choice. I don't want to be too obvious about failing. So I calculate how many I can get wrong and still look like I put in an effort. I make sure Wired can copy me.

I'm going to fail and so is he. That's payback.

The next part is short-answer questions. That's also tricky. Wired looks lost as he tries to read my sentences. I give him a look. He isn't getting it.

"Dude, you can't copy my words exactly," I whisper. "They'll know you cheated."

"Or they'll know *you* cheated," Wired hisses back. "I can tell them I saw you copying *my* page."

I stifle a laugh. That's pretty funny. Wired doesn't look amused.

As I quietly say an answer, Roberts looks our way. Did he hear me? I put my head down and scribble out a sentence. I go on to the next question and then the next before I look up again. Roberts is back to marking our final papers. Now Wired's face is full of panic.

I whisper a sentence for question number two. Then number three. He'll only have one-sentence answers. But that isn't my problem. I don't want him to pass. But I don't want to face his bodyguards, either.

Suddenly, Roberts gets up from his seat. He walks straight for us. I freeze. My pen shakes in my hand. But he passes by us and wanders through the room. Guess he's just checking on everyone's progress.

The last part of the test is a full essay question, where we have to write 500 words. I dig in and forget that I meant to fail. The stuff is everything I studied when I was into Larkyn. I remember it clearly. It feels good writing the answers. Wired begs for help with his eyes. I whisper three sentences and then say, "I'm done. You're on your own."

I take my exam to Roberts and plop it on his desk. Wired follows me. He couldn't have written the final essay question that fast. He really didn't pay attention to any of the stuff we did in class. Now I panic. The dudes who harassed me on the way in will be waiting to hear how things went. I guess I'm going to have to face Larkyn. Otherwise it won't matter how I did on the exam. I'll be getting my results from a hospital bed.

Then I'm sent back to my room for the rest of the day.

Chapter 15

Regret

I haven't had to deal with Wired or the other guys since we took the exam. Today is my birthday. I'm eighteen.

For some reason, my sixth birthday is on my mind as I lie in bed waiting for the morning to start. I remember how my mom made waffles with blueberries and whipped cream. She and I smeared whipped cream above our lips, like white moustaches, and laughed. The whole family went to Second

Beach after breakfast. As we walked, the sun made our shadows stretch out in front of us. I remember thinking how big my shadow was. I felt so tall. It was like the future was stretched out in front of me. It was like, at six, I could already see my adult self. Now I wish I could go back.

So I could get it right this time.

In the cafeteria, I choke down a breakfast of slimy eggs and white bread. I'm just about to put my tray back when I am engulfed in shadow. This time it isn't from the sun. It's from three Diablos.

"We cut you some slack because Wired said you let him copy the test," said one. "Now it's time to get Larkyn back on your roster. We've waited long enough." He pulls on my ear and practically rips it from my head.

I catch myself thinking it's a good thing we don't have our exam results back. If they knew how badly Wired did, they might have actually decapitated me.

Once back in my room, I use my desk as a drum. I pound out my frustrations on it. But I can't relax. It's like the Diablos are in my room with me. It feels like their breath is still on my neck. I turn my focus to Weed. "So how old are you? I thought spiders only lived two years. But you've stuck it out as long as me. You're trapped, too. Do you ever wish you could get out of here? Go somewhere else?"

Weed just sits in her web and doesn't move.

"Visitor," pipes Collins. I jump. I didn't know he was outside my door.

I trudge to the visitors' area. I'm not expecting anyone.

Dad says, "Hi."

I sit across from him.

"So I know this is crappy timing. But I'm going away for a few weeks."

"What! Where?" My voice has an edge to it.

"I've met someone. We're taking a trip together."

Dad's voice is different somehow. Like the person he hasn't told me about might actually mean something to him.

I wonder what would it be like to take a break from this place. To get away from the brutes down the hall. To not be constantly looking over my shoulder. The routine that used to feel comfortable in here has become harder and harder to take. Sharply, I add, "Why now?"

What I mean to say is that my dad's timing is bad. Now that my life is falling apart, I could use some support.

"Look, I'll come see you when I get back." Dad stands. A sigh slouches his body forward.

I'm not ready for the visit to be over. I have loads of questions. I have memories running around in my brain. They need answers. They need to be heard.

I feel a sense of panic. Like Dad may not return from the vacation. Like I may never get to say all the things that have been on my mind. I blurt out, "This is so typical. Just when we start to figure stuff out, you bail. You go away. That's how it was before Mom left. That's how it has been since she left."

Dad hasn't put his jacket on. He hasn't stepped away from the table. But his body is half-turned away from me. Around the room, people are talking with the inmates. But there is a hush, like they are listening to Dad and me.

"What do you want me to say?" asks Dad. "I thought maybe you'd be happy for me."

"Right. Because Martini Mason, Darlene Daiquiri, and Corona Kim made all the difference." I always called his dates by their beverage of choice, since that's mostly what they did when they came over to our house. Drink and watch TV with my dad. They weren't interested in becoming a family.

"I was hurting after your mom left. And sure, I didn't always make the best decisions. But I was trying to hold down a job and be there for you. What do you want from me?"

"Oh, right. You call what happened being there for me! Mom left and the next day you got up and went to work. You came home with dinner. After a silent meal, you watched TV until bed. The next day you got up and went to work. You came home with dinner. And the routine was set. Nothing changed. Every stinking day, we did the same thing. No talking. No figuring out what happened. Just going through the motions. Sort of like what we still do today!"

"Maybe I didn't know what to say to you." He's lowered his head.

I yell, "Okay! But you know what's really messed up about this whole thing? Maybe you didn't notice, but she left *me* too."

"I'm not responsible for decisions your mother made." Dad slumps back down into his chair.

"That leash thing you were talking about last time. I thought it was about what I did.

How that messed things up for the two of us. But now I see it could mean what happened with Mom."

Dad's silent. He wrings his hands above the table. His eyes focus on his hands. Guess that's easier than looking at me.

I'm on a roll, so I go with it. "I used to wonder why Mom left both of us. I used to ask myself at night what I did wrong."

Dad clears his throat and talks with his head lowered. "You didn't do anything wrong. Me? I made mistakes. I probably deserved it. But you didn't deserve . . . I don't know what your mom was thinking. And I don't know why she hasn't come to see you."

"Does she even know I'm in here?" Part of me hopes not. Maybe finding out what I did is what kept her away. But I know that isn't completely true. She had already been out of our lives for nearly three years when I took that car.

As we sit, no words between us, I see the pain on Dad's face.

He wants to say the same hollow words I tried to give to Aisha. But we both know sorry doesn't cut it. And since that day, I haven't been able to apologize to him. I didn't make his life easy, either.

I guess Dad has felt guilt too. Maybe he feels responsible for me losing my mom. But he never told her to skip out on me. And I know he didn't want to be stuck with me by himself.

After a few minutes of silence, the CO lets us know our time is done. Dad heads off to somewhere I can't join him.

And on his way out, he forgets to wish me a happy birthday.

Chapter 16

Reality Check

The next morning, I shake off my bad dream as soon as I open my eyes. This time, when I see the man in the snow, it isn't Aisha's dad. It's my dad.

My heart is shaking up my insides with its erratic beat. My legs are red again. I lie in bed until Collins makes me get up and start my day.

As I leave my room for the cafeteria, I spot Wired in the hall. He's walking my way. All the crap with the gang comes rushing back to me. I'm not going to be safe unless I fix this somehow.

Since I need to keep the gang and Wired off my case, I turn to Collins. "Can I talk to Jackson?" I ask my CO. "It's an emergency."

"What's the reason?"

"I need to set up a visit. Or I'll die. And I don't mean figuratively!"

Wired slows his pace like he is listening to what I'm telling Collins.

Collins and I walk to the phone and he dials Jackson's cell number. I hope Jackson answers.

Wired takes his time passing us.

My PO answers.

"Hey, Jackson," I blurt out. Then I say the next part loud enough for Wired to hear. It's for his benefit. "So when is Larkyn back on my roster? I need to see her."

It works. Wired stops and listens.

"I thought you were done with her. What's up?" asks Jackson.

"I need to confront her on some stuff. I want to clear the air. For me. Before I see Aisha. If I can't work things out with Larkyn, how can I deal with the bigger stuff Aisha and I are trying to figure out?"

I have to admit it sounds pretty good. Wired definitely buys it. He keeps walking down the hall.

"Okay," says Jackson. "I guess I can do that. Anything else on your mind?"

"Nope, that's it."

But there is a ton on my mind. Like how I am going to survive in here. If I follow through and see Larkyn, it's like I've agreed to stretch my term in juvie indefinitely. If I get caught moving contraband for Wired, the court will give me a longer sentence. I may even get my wish to go up to adult prison.

Before, I wanted to stay in because I was scared of the future. I was afraid I couldn't cut it out there. But now I am scared of what will happen if I get pulled into this gang stuff.

If I help Wired, I enter a whole new level of screwed.

I head to my room and crash on my bed. A few days ago, I had some lyrics rolling around for a song. But I can't seem to get the tune down. Not with my drum beat on the desk, not with thinking of chords for the guitar.

Then I remember something Sean said the one time the writers got to visit us. He said the hardest thing is to get the two right. To get the lyrics to match the tune, or to get the tune to match the lyrics. The essence of the two have to fit together. Then you have a hit song.

Guess that's why my life is such a mess. It's like I haven't had a 'hit song' in years. Like my dreams and goals aren't matching up with me or my life in here. And right now, it feels like they never will. Like I'm stuck. Stuck in this place. Stuck in a crazy loop with my dad, with Wired, with myself. I think about everything I'm doing right now. Giving Wired money to keep him off my back. Giving in to see Larkyn so I can move contraband and keep the gangs away. All of it is just going to spiral out of control. It isn't going to get better.

It's only going to get worse.

And to top it all off, I'm pretty sure I failed the History exam. I've been failing in every other part of my life. At least I am keeping it consistent. I get my $25 pay for cleaning the gym. I pocket it until the next time I see Wired. It's his now, anyway.

The only good thing about today is that we finally get to see the writers again. I'm looking forward to it. It's an hour where I won't have anyone staring me down. No one pushing me. No one giving me a hard time about what my future looks like if I don't do as I'm told.

***

When it's time, I head to the room where we meet with the writers. As usual, Macaroni and I are the first two there. It's grey day today, so we're both in grey sweats. Macaroni motions for me to sit beside him. I do.

"Hey, Strider," he says. "Get anything done on your song?"

"Not really. It's been a tough week."

"Yeah, the lockdown and all."

At least he doesn't go off on me.

"I didn't mind being stuck on my own. It meant no one could harass me," he continues. "I took the poetry session last time. The dude introduced us to Shane Koyczan. Know him?"

"No . . . Wait. Is he that guy at the 2010 Olympics?" I remember an English teacher talking about him, how poetry made the big stage.

"Yeah. That's the guy. Well, his slam poem 'To This Day' really hit me. I mean, it's my story. Only I got back at the bullies, and it landed me in here. So I just hurt myself more. Know what I mean?"

"I guess." The writers are filing in. Sean waves at me. I hope he doesn't expect a lot since the last time we were together.

"Well," Macaroni goes on, chewing on his nail. "I have a full poem ready to go. One that talks about the bullies. The guys who made my life miserable. The guys who got me so riled up I did something . . . something that got me sentenced to this place. This place is one hundred times worse than out there. I wish I never . . ."

I look at Macaroni. I really see him for the first time. He's just a lost, scared kid who finally got back at the jerks who gave him crap. Only to trade that for bigger jerks who make things even worse for him. He screwed up too. Everyone in here has screwed up. Some worse than others. But we're all looking for the same thing — a little peace. Just a little peace.

And that's the last thing we get in here.

As the afternoon goes on, Sean gives me cool tips for song writing. Mostly we just jam some tunes on the guitars. It's an hour where

I almost forget where I am. But before I know it, the guards are calling "Time." I drag myself down the hall. Back in my room I work on Strummer's song.

Chapter 17

Second Chance

It's Saturday and we are all allowed to chill in our rooms. After breakfast and chores, I return to my room. I want to hammer out more lyrics for Strummer's song. I'm just in the middle of a great line when I am interrupted by Collins.

"You have a visitor."

"What? But my dad is out of town." I'm kind of surprised.

As I approach the visitors' area, I see through the window that it's Aisha. She's back. My PO didn't give me a heads up. I'm not ready to meet with her. I haven't planned what to say.

But since I am already here, I approach the table. I pull out a chair and slide into it. Everything that happened this past month bubbles to the surface. Aisha's eyes take in my mangled face. Before she can say anything, my words are spilling out. "Why did you come back? I bailed on you. I didn't expect you to want to reach out again."

"No, I blew it last time. I was so nervous meeting you. I didn't know how I would react. I didn't know if I could keep my emotions in check. I didn't sleep the night before."

"I didn't sleep, either." I don't tell her I never sleep well. Any night. "But I get it. Almost being hit as you drove in, that . . . I . . ." My voice trails off.

She looks as though she might put her hand over mine. I panic. First, because I don't want the guards to freak out and act like they usually do about touching the visitors. But also because I don't know why she would extend that kind of peace offering.

"Maybe because I was tired," she says, "it hit me harder when that guy ran the stop sign. But after you left the visitors' area, I had to sit with my feelings. All my feelings around confronting you. And I had to look at what happened on my way in to see you that day. I thought about what the man was doing when he ran the stop sign. Not paying attention. That's his error." She looks at me. Her brown eyes are scared, but soft at the same time. "Last year, do you remember how we had that huge dump of snow? Well, on my way to university, I was going slowly. I was being careful. But I still slid through a stop sign because I hit black ice. My professor is from Winnipeg and he says drivers there grow up with this stuff. They know to pump the brakes. They gear down. They have tricks that make them better drivers under those conditions. I could have slid into someone. Like you slid into . . ."

Now her eyes fill with tears again. I think of what Jackson said. I'm responsible for being an idiot and jumping in the car. Could I have slid on ice as a new driver once I was legal to drive? Yeah, I guess.

I find some courage. Out loud I say, "But I created the scenario that put me on that ice without driving experience. Without legally being able to drive. I'm the one who did that. I'm responsible for being behind the wheel when that happened."

Now *my* emotions spill out. I feel foolish having tears run down my cheeks. But I press on. Aisha is hanging on every word I say. "Every single day, I wake up regretting my actions. I wish I had walked past that car. I wish I hadn't thought the police car was after me. I wish I could take that day back. Then I could give you back your life the way it was. Your dad . . ."

"But that's the part you need to know," Aisha cuts in. "He survived the crash. Sure, his legs were damaged for a long time. But after a year and a half of rehab, he started walking again. He still uses a cane, but things could have been worse. My dad is celebrating being alive."

I feel a sliver of relief. Of course I knew he wasn't dead. But for two and a half years, I've felt like I took his life. I mean I did, in a way. He couldn't walk.

Aisha continues. "Dad says this was a blessing. He didn't like his old job. And because he had to change careers due to his legs, he now has a job he loves — working in a library."

My chest heaves while Aisha is talking.

"And I'm happy," she says. "I'm happy my dad is in a better place. I'm happy because I just got engaged to a man I met at university. We want to get married, have children, and pursue our careers. But I realize that to do all of that, I have to have a clear heart. A heart that isn't blackened by a tragedy from the past.

I have been hanging on to hate and anger. My heart was heavy because of it. I already feel lighter just meeting with you."

I nod. My heart has been dark too. And these last few weeks, with Larkyn and Wired and the Diablos, it was blackening even more.

Aisha puts her hand up as though she could wipe away my sadness. Then she points at my eye and cut lip. "What happened, Kevin?"

"It was nothing."

She looks concerned. "I thought youth custody would be more like a learning environment than a prison."

"Ha!" I laugh. But she doesn't join me. So she won't freak out, I add, "It's not as bad as it looks."

"I wanted you to be punished, Kevin. But this isn't what I expected. I don't know what the answer is. But it isn't this."

"Look," I say, as everything hits me at once. "I was told that I could be released early.

But I don't want that. I need to do all the time they give me. Even if it means going up to adult prison. I messed up your dad's life. I messed up your life. I deserve this."

"No Kevin, not this." She looks around us before speaking again. "I'm not sure this is teaching you anything." Her voice softens. "Tell me something. What did you learn from what happened that day?"

"That being impulsive is stupid. I mean, I just wish I had thought things through. I wish I hadn't jumped into the car without thinking of the consequences. But I didn't know I'd slide through the intersection. I didn't know someone would be crossing the street at just that moment. But it really makes no difference, does it? The car wasn't mine. I had no license. I shouldn't have done it. And every day when I wake up, my first thoughts are of your dad. I'm sorry for hurting him. For hurting you . . ."

Aisha takes in my words. She sits and lets what I've said sink in.

Then she smiles at me.

Until this moment, I had no idea how huge one small act — one smile — could be. Her smile. Something I never thought I would get to see. My cheeks flush. Then we talk until our time is up.

After the visit, I head back to my room. My step is lighter than it has been in two and a half years. In even longer than that. Since Mom left. My door opens. I enter the room. The heavy door closes behind me.

I walk to my bed and sit down. Then my eyes roam to my desk, where a stack of papers sits for studying and song writing. On top of the white paper is a crumpled little ball of black. I take a closer look and I realize it's Weed.

And she's dead.

I lay my head down next to her.

Chapter 18

Moving On

A few days after the visit with Aisha, I am still processing everything she said. It is taking me a long time to shift my focus. But I'm beginning to move away from fear of what life might be like outside this joint, to seeing that I have been punishing myself for what I did to Aisha's dad. Ever since the day my guilt flowed out like hot lava, I have been struggling to get my feelings in check. That's probably why I blew up on my dad. It's probably why I failed the test on purpose, screwing up my chance to graduate. But the worst part is that I am now caught up with this gang stuff. And I don't have Wired on my side anymore.

Collins comes by my room to tell me there is a phone call. I don't know who it could be. I walk to the phone, half worried, and say, "Hello?"

Collins stands next to me so he can hear every word I say.

"Hey, Strider, it's Strummer," I hear.

Relief fills me. I say, "How are you doing, man? I'm glad you called."

"I'm . . . okay. Better than you."

"You heard?" My hand rubs under my eye where the bruise is still puffy.

"Yeah, news like that travels. What the hell happened?"

"I'm handling it. It's all good." But my voice betrays me.

"Listen, I called for one reason," he says. "And I was only allowed to call because Jackson arranged this. For your benefit. My CO is listening at this end."

I look at Collins. He is standing with his feet apart, legs stretched out. It's the stance he takes when he means business.

Strummer's voice echoes through the phone. "I called to tell you to stay out of it. Don't get involved with the gang. Once you do, you never get out. They'll pull you back in."

It's like he read my mind. It's all I have been thinking about.

Strummer's tone is grave. "The gang is priming you. This is real. You'll get in deep the moment you say yes to anything they ask. Trust me. I've been there."

He's right. I know it. But I don't like my face being used as a canvas for their fist-painting. "Got any ideas on how to do what you're asking?" I say into the phone. "It's not that easy."

"I know. That's how I ended up in here.

You think juvie is hard? It's nothing compared to this. We may not have the death penalty in Canada, but it doesn't matter. Over half the guys in here have put a death sentence on themselves. I'm so done with this joint. If anything will help me get through my time, it's knowing *you* get things on track and get out. Do you hear me? I need you to get out. And I need you to make it out there."

His words hit me hard. I throw it right back at him. "Why don't you do that for yourself? You can make it. I know you can. The two of us could hang out. We could maybe even write some songs." As I say it, I know it won't happen.

"I've talked to some dudes. They know the guys who are giving you grief. The guys there will back off. You know what I mean?"

I read between the lines. Strummer is saying that he knows some guys who can get to the gang members. In here. In juvie! Guys who can put pressure on them to leave me alone.

But he can't say it directly with the guards listening.

Strummer can tell from my silence that I've figured it out. "Just keep your head down and stay out of trouble," he says.

"But how can you . . . What will you have to do?" I cringe thinking about what might happen to Strummer if he helps me.

"Let's just say I made the right kind of friends while I was out. Listen, I have to go. Keep writing. Finish the song you and I started."

The click of the phone is loud in my ear, like a door slamming shut. A door that might never open again.

Even though the line is silent, Strummer's words ring in my ears.

I think about how everyone is moving on. My dad. Aisha and her dad. Even Strummer. Weed is gone too. Seems like the universe is telling me something.

Aisha has extended her hand to me. A

hand that reaches to me from the future. A future that maybe doesn't have to be as bleak as I thought. Not with her leaning toward forgiveness. If she can forgive me, can I forgive Wired? After all, he's just trying to survive in here. My life was better when we hung out. Before he lost his privileges. Wired is doing what he has to. That's the system he's a part of, and it won't change.

Larkyn-with-a-backwards-*k* gave me a gift. Even though things got royally screwed up, she made me think of a future. Something after this place.

I don't want to hang out with Larkyn. I can't trust her. But I guess I can cut her some slack. She was just looking out for her brother. The bigger question is if I can cut myself some slack. Or is it too late?

A song idea pops into my head.

Too late for you and me. Too late for an apology. But too late for moving on? My old life is said and done. What matters now is stepping out.

Making time and losing doubt . . .

Kind of lame, but it's a start. The chords are in my head. The percussion beats through my knuckles on the desk. It's the first time words and a beat are coming together. They need work, but it feels right.

I think of Aisha getting married. Marriage isn't on my radar. Hell, it wouldn't be, even if I were out. But after Larkyn, I know I want something real with the right girl. Maybe with someone like Tanika.

I see us going to concerts. We could hang out at clubs, listening to local bands. Dancing. Kissing. None of that is possible in here. Making music isn't possible here. But if I was out, I could see if the guys I used to jam with are still playing. Maybe they'd have a spot for me in their band. If they still have one.

For any of this to happen, for me to have any kind of future, I need to give Aisha more than I have so far. She came to see me for a reason. She expects something from me. And now I think I can give her what she needs. For real. I feel it in my insides. This tingling feeling that runs through my fingers. It's like creating a song.

I know what to do. I will write her a letter. Something more than just the words I speak. I'll give her those, too, so she can hear that I mean it. But a letter is something she can come back to, something she can read over again whenever she feels doubt. Whenever she doubts that I regret my actions that day.

I look at the calendar by my desk. The writers are coming in two days. I'll work with Sean on tuning a letter, rather than a song. For now, that will be my focus. And if Strummer is true to his word, the guys will be laying off.

Then I can focus on something other than just surviving every day.

Chapter 19

PTSD

I don't know what Strummer did, but for the next couple of days, the dudes leave me alone. They still knock into me when they pass me in the halls. They still stare me down in the cafeteria. But they aren't laying into me and causing major damage.

I call Jackson to let him know I was putting on an act for Wired. Jackson says he'd figured that out. He tells me he put Larkyn's visits to me on hold. It's a stall tactic, but one that buys us time. And Wired is buying it. Jackson told him the last time Larkyn visited, things got ugly. That he's just keeping us all safe.

I put some effort into studying for my other exams. The ones I'm not so keen on. History was my ticket to do well. I blew it. I hope I don't mess up on my other tests. Especially now that I want to move forward. I want to move slowly, but forward all the same.

To be sure I keep the dudes off my back, I'm helping Wired prepare for the English and Math exams. He doesn't need much help with Math. He's pretty good with numbers, especially big ones. I'm glad he takes my help, though, as the Diablos spend a lot of time watching us.

The day before the English exam, I call Jackson and ask him to meet with me. I tell him I think I might be ready to apply for early parole. He's stoked. He sets up our time for the morning. When Collins comes for me, he leads me into a private room. Jackson is waiting with a lady.

"This is Ms. Strong. She's a social worker, Kevin. She can help with your application for probation."

"Hello, Kevin," says Ms. Strong. "Nice to meet you."

In the past, I've cringed when someone said that. *Nice to meet you.* It's always sounded fake. But this lady seems sincere.

"So, Kevin," she says. "Tell me about what happened. And where you are now. This will give us an idea of how to present to the board."

I begin with that day. As I share what happened, like always, the vision is right in front of me. I begin to shake. Ms. Strong puts her hand on my shoulder. Jackson doesn't stop her.

"You know," she says, "Their family suffered trauma. The man you hit lost the use of his legs for a long time. He lost his job. They were all hurt by your actions."

I nod. "I know."

"But have you ever thought about yourself? You were involved in the crash too. You bashed your head against the steering wheel. You got out of the car and saw him lying there. What were your first thoughts then? Do you recall?"

They never leave me. "I thought he was dead. I thought I had killed . . ." Suddenly, I can't breathe. "Sorry, can I go?"

I stand up. Nervous energy courses through my legs to my feet.

Ms. Strong turns to my PO and says, "Mr. Jackson, could you please get Kevin some water?"

Jackson leaves the room and Ms. Strong turns back to me. "Are you feeling the same sense of panic you did that day, Kevin? The same dread for what you saw?"

"Yeah," I manage to choke out. I stand behind my chair, my arms on the back of it to keep me balanced. "I wake up to the same image and feelings every morning. Some days it takes a long time to get my body to stop shaking. To stop the feelings of fear before I can even get out of bed. I used to think my legs were paralyzed, just like his."

"That makes a lot of sense," Ms. Strong replies. "It's normal to relive these feelings. Maybe we can help you work them out."

At that moment, Jackson returns to the room. He places a cup of water in front of me. I gulp it down fast. I think of what Ms. Strong just said. She's right. I experienced trauma too. And I haven't worked through it. I didn't have anyone helping me to deal with my feelings before.

As she leaves, Ms. Strong lets me know she will visit once a week, so we can talk.

✳✳✳

We have back-to-back exams. I let Wired copy me again. This time he doesn't look over as often. It makes it easier to keep us both out of trouble. I think Wired actually took in some of my tutoring. Good thing, because Roberts paces the room a lot more this time.

After two days of tests, I hear that my dad is back from his vacation. And that he wants to see me.

Dad's already waiting at a table for me when I get to the visitors' area. I'm in all blue today. He's wearing a shirt with Hawaiian flowers on it. I guess Hawaii is where he went.

"How was your trip?" I ask. There's no trace of attitude in my voice.

"Good. Lacey and I . . . The vacation was good. Especially the weather. Except there was a volcano. We were at Kilauea, but the ash from the fallout affected us. Still, we had a good time."

Volcanoes. Ash. Fallout.

My volcanic feelings blew weeks ago. Now maybe it's time for Dad and me to talk about the fallout.

"Dad," I start, "I saw Aisha. The daughter of the man I hit that day. We've been talking."

"I heard. Jackson let me know. That's a big step. I'm glad you're finally taking responsibility and all."

"Finally?" How can he not know I've felt sorry since the moment it happened? I feel the usual tension tightening my body.

But Dad is in another place and doesn't notice. "I haven't felt this good since your mom and I split up. Something you said last time I saw you really hit me. That you suffered too. You lost your mom. And because I was struggling with everything, you lost out on time with me. I mean quality time. I was there, going through the motions, just like you said, Kevin. But that was it."

Dad lowers his head. I want to move forward. I want things to be better between us. But it's hard. I decide to let things go for now. Dad and I have work to do and it will take some time to figure things out. To trust again. So I change the subject. "Where was Gemini while you were gone?" I ask.

"Lacey's daughter looked after him. She has a Husky too. Gemini and her dog get along. But Gemini still sleeps in your room every night. At the foot of your bed. He's waiting for you."

I get up and head to the pop machine. I don't want my dad to see my cheeks flush because I miss my dog. For the rest of our visit we talk about Dad's vacation. I think about Gemini and what it would be like to be home again.

Chapter 20

The Letter

On Sunday the writers come. Sean helps me work on a letter for Aisha. Later, as I lie in bed reading over the letter, things that Jackson and the social worker talked about strike a chord. Maybe before my dad and Aisha can forgive me, I need to learn how to forgive myself. That's going to take a lot of work and a lot of effort. So I start by saying, "I'm sorry."

This time, the words are just for me.

* * *

Jackson is standing in the room with me as we
wait for Aisha to arrive. He has to be there. I'm
not allowed to pass the letter to her myself. In
fact, Jackson has to read it first, to approve it.
It's weird, but Jackson actually gets emotional
as he reads it.

The letter is shaking in his hand. "I don't
know if you know this, Kevin," he says. "I have
a son. He's twenty-eight. We went through a
tough patch. After reading this, it makes me
grateful that he and I made it. That everything
worked out."

I don't know why he's telling me this. Is
it his way of saying everything will work out
with Aisha? It sounds like he thinks the letter is
going to help.

Jackson picks a table near the window. It's
the first time I've ever sat at this table. This
close to the window, the day looks bright.
It's June, so I bet it's warm out. Just as we get

seated, Aisha enters the visitors' area. She's wearing a print dress with flowers on it.

Once she is sitting at the table with us, Jackson says, "Kevin wrote this letter for you. I have to read it out loud. And then you may take it from me to keep."

This is the part I can do without. I want to be able to hand things to people myself. To take care of things on my own. But I swallow my frustration so I can be in the moment, as Aisha takes in my words to her.

Jackson's voice falters as he reads my letter:

"I am glad that your dad is happy with his new job at the library. But it shouldn't have happened this way. *It shouldn't have been* because I hurt him. He shouldn't have had to deal with rehab and hospitals and court cases. He shouldn't have had to make a decision about work until he was ready to make that decision on his own. *It should have been* because he wanted a change. Not because he had to change jobs. I took that choice away from him."

While Jackson reads, I keep my eyes on Aisha. My PO keeps sharing my words:

"I am sorry that I took your father away from you and your brother while he healed in the hospital. You were in your teens, just like me, and needed your dad. Just like I needed mine."

As Jackson reads, I realize that the word *sorry* doesn't have to be small. I can make it bigger by showing my true feelings. I nod when Jackson reads the important parts, to emphasize my words.

Aisha keeps her head down for some time after Jackson finishes reading. I remember how he said I don't have to say anything. I can just listen. So I wait.

Her voice is shaky when she begins talking. As she looks into my eyes, hers are glazed with tears. "Thank you, Kevin. You're right. I was hurt and angry that Dad was away for so long. I needed him home during my senior year as I planned my future. He was my rock. I felt lost without him. But I also learned to be more independent because he wasn't there.

"My brother started going down the wrong path. He was angry and full of hate for what you did. He made some mistakes too. Because he was acting out of anger. But I learned that we have a good family system. My uncle stepped in and spent time with my brother when my dad was in the hospital. My uncle helped my brother get back on track. My mom is still angry. She isn't ready to meet with you. Nor is my brother. They'll have to come to that place on their own. If they ever do. I hope they do. I don't like seeing their hearts so dark.

"My dad still has trouble walking. It makes me sad to see him this way, but with a cane he gets around. That would have come with age, but it happened sooner than it should have. It hurts to watch him, especially on days when he feels more pain.

"But I'm here because I want to be here. I want to move forward." She wipes away the tears and smiles again. "I accept your letter, Kevin. And I hope we can talk some more?"

"Sure," I say. "I want to hear more about how this has been for you. If your mom or your brother want to come talk to me, I will listen."

"And how about my dad?"

I take a deep breath. Seeing him will be hard, for sure. But I can do it if it will help. "I'll see your dad. If he wants to see me."

"Good," she smiles. "Because he definitely wants to meet you."

"Really?" I'm surprised.

Jackson is grinning from ear to ear.

Aisha leans in. "It's my dad's birthday today. Can I read him your letter as part of his present?"

"Sure. I mean . . . if you think it will help?"

"I do. And thank you, Kevin. For letting me say what I needed to say today. I have more to share. But we have time. We have time to heal. You and me."

And me.

Aisha has included me in her message. I have time to heal. There is a ton to heal from. But this feels like a start.

Chapter 21

Waiting

Three months have passed. Today is the day I finally speak to the parole board. For the first time since I've been in here, I don't wake up shaking from reliving the accident. Instead, I wake up with Gemini on my mind.

Jackson picks me up for the parole hearing. I am dressed in black pants and a white button-up shirt.

"Looking slick," says my PO. "I think you're ready."

As he drives us to the meeting, we review some of the things I will say.

"Be sure to tell them you passed all your exams," he says.

I interrupt. "Barely passed the History test." I lucked out and got a C.

"Right. But be sure to add that you graduated. I brought the picture of you and your dad standing together with you in your cap and gown."

"Thanks," I say, looking out the window. I haven't been on the outside for a long time. It feels weird. Weird enough that I almost change my mind. We pass a bus stop. Everyone is lined up waiting for the bus to the university. Some have headphones in their ears, listening to music. Others are scrolling through their cell phones or laughing with each other. They are doing things people on the outside do daily. Things I haven't done in three years.

Jackson must sense that I'm stressing. "It will be okay," he says. "Just share what has happened in the last few months. You've got this."

A while later we arrive at the courthouse. Jackson and I are escorted to a room. There we meet with Ms. Strong and three other people who will help to decide my fate.

They don't throw a bunch of questions at me. Instead, they suggest I just focus on the things that have happened recently that show I am ready to be on parole.

I begin with the easy stuff. Things that don't get me too wound up. "I took a creative writing course. And Sean, the dude I worked with, got me thinking about post-secondary education. I found a college that has song writing, sound design, and sound engineering, all in one. It seems like a perfect fit. Sean is helping me with my application."

Two of the parole board members nod. I think that means I'm on the right track. So I go on. "I added extra chores to my weekly jobs. And this new guy came in last week. He kind

of reminds me of myself back at fifteen, except he's only thirteen."

I find myself wringing my hands like my dad. I'm nervous and my mouth is dry. A jug and some glasses sit in the middle of the table. I nod my head toward the water. One of the men passes me a glass and then motions for me to take the jug. I pour the water and swig it quickly. Licking my dry lips, I take up my story again. "So, like I said, this kid is only thirteen. I decided to help him out, like Strummer helped me when I first came in to juvie. We nicknamed the kid Charlie Brown."

I smile thinking about how good it feels to help someone else. To not just be focused on myself. "He's into fantasy writing. Vampires, dark lords, that kind of stuff. So I invited him to hang out with us when the writers are here."

"And what kind of writing did you say you are doing?" asks Ms. Strong.

"Song writing. But I want to produce songs too. I've got a goal."

Jackson smiles. He primed me for this part of the application.

"And what else would you like to share?" The third guy asks. He chews on the end of his pencil while he waits to hear more of my story. As soon as I begin speaking, his pencil scratches across the page as he takes notes.

I'm getting to the tough stuff now. "It's still rough with my dad, but getting better. It's hard to work things out in twenty-minute visits, every two weeks. And I meet with Aisha once a week now, to work on a plan with her to make amends to her family. She figures when I get out, I can help her family with renovations on their house. Things her dad can't do as easily now."

The guy's eyes bore into mine. "And what about her dad? The man you harmed in the accident. Have you talked to him?"

"Yeah, I met with Aisha's dad. It was hard to see him walk in with a cane. But I can see where Aisha gets her smile from. Her dad

said I can make amends by painting the deck off the kitchen. He's happy that I want to fix things. And he told me he has lots of things for me to fix."

I look up. The parole board members are nodding.

I keep this next part to myself. They don't need to hear this. I've thought a lot about my mom. I will probably never see her. Dad doesn't have a forwarding address for her. I realized that I have a lot of anger stored up toward her for how she has hurt me. I need to let that go. Waiting for her to make contact, to come back has been eating me up. It's also added a lot of tension between my dad and me. I have to move forward.

I want to move forward.

I look at each person at the table as I finish. "I guess the last thing I need to share with you is how sorry I am for everything that happened that day. I never thought in a million years that taking that car would mean hurting

an innocent pedestrian on his way to work. That was not my intention. But it happened. I have taken responsibility for my actions. And both he and his daughter are on the road to forgiving me. I know this is just the beginning. There is still a ton of healing to be done, but I'm ready to do the work. All of it."

Now there is nothing I can do but wait.

Wait to see if I convinced the parole board that I'm on the right track. Wait to see if they believe I will not be a menace to society. Wait to see if they believe I regret my past actions and that I'm truly on a better path. I will wait to see if, three years to the day, I am granted early release.